Sea, Swallow Me

and other stories

Sea, Swallow Me

and other stories

Craig Laurance Gidney

Lethe Press

Maple Shade, NJ

This trade paperback published by Lethe Press
118 Heritage Ave, Maple Shade, NJ 08052
www.lethepressbooks.com
lethepress@aol.com

Printed in the United States of America

Book Design by Toby Johnson
Cover art by Thomas Drymon

First U.S. edition, 2008
ISBN 1-59021-066-2   978-1-59021-066-6

"The Safety of Thorns" first appeared 2005 in *Say… Have You Heard This One*
"Her Spirit Hovering" first appeared 2003 in the literary journal *Riprap*
"Sea, Swallow Me" first appeared 2006 in *Ashé Journal*
"Circus Boy Without A Safety Net" first appeared 2001 in *Spoonfed*
"Magpie Sisters" first appeared 2007 in the online journal *Serendipity*
"A Bird of Ice" first appeared 2007 in *So Fey: Queer Fairy Fiction*

Library of Congress Cataloging-in-Publication Data

Gidney, Craig Laurance, 1967-
 Sea, swallow me and other stories / Craig Laurance Gidney. -- 1st U.S. ed.
    p. cm.
 ISBN 1-59021-066-2
 1. Magic--Fiction. 2. Fantasy fiction, American. 3. American fiction--African American authors. 4. Gays' writings, American. I. Title. II.
Title: Sea, swallow me.
 PS3607.I275S43 2008
 813'.6--dc22

                                2008041282

To My Parents

Stories

The Safety of Thorns

Israel Jones first saw the Devil on Saturday night, rising out of the briar patch that was at the edge of Moonflower, the Joneses' plantation. The cruel thorns of the briar patch parted, releasing a swarm of mosquitoes and a man-shaped thing. Nothing, of course, could live there, except for insects—the mosquitoes, flies and biting nits. Old Scratch dusted himself off, and picked off burrs from his suit, which was the color of kudzu. He was crowned with a black silk top hat that boasted a white feather. There was no mistaking him. His skin was as black as tar, a color that glistened, but did not reflect. His face was a beautiful, if inhuman mask. His skin looked as if it were made of a magical wood, one that possessed fluid properties. He had a guitar dangling from one hand. His fingernails were curved but clean. He walked across the top of the briar patch gracefully, not quite a parody of the Lord walking across the waters.

"Hey, boy," he called out. His voice was husky, but surprisingly gentle. "What are you doing out on a night like this?"

Israel didn't answer at first.

"What's the matter," the Devil asked, concerned. "Are you a mute?"

Israel shook his head. But he wasn't sure if the stranger could see in the dark, so he said, "No, sir. I'm just running an errand for Master Rufus." He didn't mention that the "errand" was to buy some moonshine from Cletus, who lived at the edge of the swamp.

The Devil just nodded. "Do me a favor," he said. "Hold this for a moment." He handed the guitar to Israel. He hesitantly accepted the instrument, fret board first. Even in the feeble light of a half moon, he could see that it was no ordinary guitar. The hourglass body of the guitar was intricately inlaid with designs, in tones of ruby, sapphire and mother-of-pearl. At first glance they seemed to be abstract. But on closer inspection, Israel could make out shapes, human-like forms that shimmered back into vagueness. Jeweled faces were caught in the wood. These must be the trapped souls he harvested.

The Devil reached into his jacket pocket, and produced a cheroot. With a snap of the fingers, the tip of the cheroot was sparked. He put it in his mouth. "The wife," he said after blowing out a plume of smoke, "she don't like it when I smoke down there. So I gotta do it out here."

Its smell was sweet and spicy, kind of like cinnamon, not at all like those nasty pipes that Master Rufus smoked. Isabel, the slave in charge of the female slaves (or Queen Field Nigger, as she was known) swore that he smoked dung mixed with tobacco. "Nothing but mule shit."

"The Devil has a wife?" The words were out of his mouth before he could stop them.

The Devil laughed at that, his teeth dangerous pearls. It was a dark sound, full of earthworms and the chittering wings of insects. "Boy," he said when he was done, "I ain't the devil. My wife might think differently, though."

"Then who are you?"

The cheroot tip glowed a good, long while before he took a drag. The expelled smoke curled to the sky. Israel could swear there were faces in the smoke that broke apart as drifted upwards.

"Call me Earl. Earl King."

Should he run? And where to? It seemed stupid to continue with Master Rufus' errand, as if nothing had happened. And yet, to return empty-handed wasn't without risk.

"Boy, you're thinking too hard," said Mr. King. (King of Hell, no doubt). "Now, I said I wasn't the Devil."

Israel nodded, moving away. "Ain't no reason to be afraid," Mr. King repeated.

He bolted toward Moonflower's gate, kicking up dust. Stars, clouds, grass all swirled past him. His dungarees would be filthy when he got back home. It was a queer thought to have, when he was running for his life. He didn't get very far. A viselike grip stopped him.

"Please, please sir, don't hurt me. I'm a good Christian."

"I don't care if you're a good Christian or not," Mr. King calmly informed him. "I just want my guitar back."

Israel wasn't aware that he still had it. But sure enough, the iridescent instrument was in his clutch.

Israel handed it over to him, quaking. As soon as the guitar was in Mr. King's hand, he was let go. His body tensed for flight, but he held back. The figures on the guitar mesmerized him. Leaves became faces became waves became wings. They resolved into a face, of sorts, with the hole in the hourglass' center being the mouth. Two leaf-green eyes blinked at him from the hollow body. The eyes were feminine and full of warmth. They had the sparkle that he imagined a mother had for her child. This soul, at least, didn't appear to be trapped. But it could be a trick. Mr. King calmly observed him.

"Would you like me to play a song for you?"

Israel, mute with wonder, nodded.

Mr. King held the guitar against his body, and a strap appeared, a fabric-snake of night and stars. It slithered over his body, attaching and balancing the instrument. The first chord struck was clear and brittle, like Moonflower's tobacco fields beneath an icing of frost. Mr. King's voice harmonized with the guitar, in a deeper tone. The song he sang was a short one, unlike the gospel songs that the other slaves sang, or the hymns of the masters. This song was dark and hot, the sulfur stink of the bayou in it. It oozed over him, like soft black mud at the bottom of a creek. Yet, there was a beauty to it as well, with lilies afloat above the muck, the hot eyes of the raccoon, watching. There were words to the song, words he tried to hold onto, but they escaped like mist. At the end, Israel only had a sensation in the pit of his belly, and fading images of moonlight spilled across water, the slick jade of leaping frogs, the filmy laziness of catfish. He saw the crumbling colors of the bayou: brown, blue and green. When the song finished, Israel found his eyes moist.

The guitar-girl fluttered her lashes in sympathy.

Mr. King smiled. His teeth glowed, starlight captured in a crescent. "She likes you."

Her eyes laughed in agreement.

"What's her name?"

"It's getting late, boy. Best be on your way back, before your master gets suspicious."

Israel, turned, heading for the gate. He'd surely be whipped, if he didn't get that moonshine from Cletus.

"Son, there ain't no reason to be going to that shack in the middle of the bayou." Mr. King reached into his bulgeless left pocket and withdrew a long bottle that couldn't possibly been hidden there. The liquid within was fiery white and translucent. It stilled into a deadly clearness, with a faint green tint. Israel took the bottle from his hands. It was cold, the bottle. There was a purple-green label on it, scrawled with the finest script Israel had ever seen. He couldn't read, but he wanted to very badly at that moment.

"Thank you, sir," he said.

Mr. King nodded. "I best be going," he said. "The wife…"

He melted into the night, color spilling out, tar-face painting itself onto the night. The last impression left were the giggling green eyes of the guitar girl.

Israel walked up the dusty road, in one of the ruts left by the many carriages that visited Moonflower. His own father, long dead, was rumored to be one of the Joneses' coachmen until he up and tried to escape. Israel walked around the front entrance of the manse, which was lantern-lit in the dark. White rhododendron bushes competed with dark magenta azaleas. The front porch of the house was empty; a porch swing creaked in the gentle summer breeze. The pale emerald liquid in the bottle sparkled in the moonlight. Israel hid the bottle under his ratty jacket; it wouldn't do to let Sr. Master Jones catch him with hooch. Master Rufus wouldn't protect him, not when his own honor was at stake. In a side window, he caught a glimpse of the lady of house. She was sickly, had that scarlet fever a few years back and never recovered. A tree of candles illuminated her, as she read the Bible.

The path to the slave shacks was dark and muddy. The first shack, not much more than a lean-to, was a few feet away from the white folks' fancy outhouse, with its tin roof and carved crescent moon on the door. The smell of shit hung in the air, along with the stinks of animal dung, lime and human sweat. Vengeful flies eddied around him briefly. Tansy lived in the third shack from the outhouse.

Israel knocked softly and entered. Tansy's mother, Bertha, sat in darkness in a rocking chair. She was as blind as a bat, her eyes a milky gray. She rocked by the stove, covered in shawls in spite of the heat. A kerosene lantern lay by bed at the opposite end of the room, casting light on the business at hand. Master Rufus's pale, freckled buttocks shivered. Tansy knelt before him, her golden-brown arms encircling his waist. His hands were entwined in her thick hair, yanking her face forward.

He muttered under his breath: "…take it, black bitch…"

Bertha continued rocking. Was she smiling? Israel caught the beginnings of a smirk, as if she were laughing at a private joke. Maybe she was deaf as well.

Master Rufus gripped Tansy's face, as he shuddered. He swore, but he did not seem angry. When Master Rufus withdrew from her mouth, his wet thing dribbled. He pulled up his pants in a fluid motion.

He turned around and grinned sheepishly. "Boy, you creep up all silent-like, like a cat."

"Sorry, sir," Israel replied.

"Ain't no reason be sorry. I like your stealth—"

Retching interrupted Master Rufus. Tansy bent over the wood floor, a frothed line of spittle joining a small puddle. She coughed.

Master Rufus knelt over her. "What's the matter, Tansy? Don't like my taste?" He rubbed her shoulders.

"L'il cat," Master Rufus said, beckoning him over. "You got my stuff? Good, bring it here."

Israel handed him the bottle, with its spectral liquid. Master Rufus uncapped it, and handed it Tansy. "Here, drink," he said.

She looked at the bottle with suspicion.

"I said drink it, gal. That's an order."

She took a cautious sip. Of course the moonshine would burn whatever taste she had in mouth. Both he and Master Rufus tensed up for her spitting the hooch out. But it didn't happen. Instead, Tansy took a long swig, as if it were the purest water. Master Rufus' face changed from mischievous to annoyed. He snatched the bottle away from the girl.

"What are you, a drunk? This stuff costs good money." He snarled, and took a defiant swig himself. He immediately spat it out, clutching his throat. His pale face turned beet-red, and water poured from his closed eyes. Both Tansy and Israel endured his coughing for several minutes.

"Damn," he said when he surfaced from the fit, "that stuff's strong. Like goddamn kerosene."

As soon as he could stand, Master Rufus left them in a huff, slamming the door to the shack. Bertha's rocking rhythm was undisturbed.

"He left his 'shine," Israel said.

Tansy stared at it, left in the center of the floor. The liquid was bright, pale silver-green. "Izzy," she said. "Taste it."

"Naw," he said, fingering the right strap of his suspenders.

"Please," Tansy said. "Just a sip." Her eyes were large and moist. They glowed, with the same luminescence that the liquid the bottle had. The green eyes of the devil man and the soul trapped in the guitar were distilled in the bottle. But it wasn't a poisonous green but the pale of young leaves.

One sip, and he'd be damned forever. No pearly gates, no river of milk, no meals of honey for him. He knew it, and somehow he didn't care.

He picked up the bottle, still cool in this hot summer night, and paused. He put the bottle to his lips, and took a tiny sip. It was sweet and cold, and had the faint taste of honeysuckle. It went down as smooth as cream, coating his throat, his stomach, his soul in sweet soft velvet.

"Izzy," said Tansy, after he'd finished. "What did you taste?" She gently prized the bottle from his hands.

Israel thought for a moment. "Summer," he said. Tansy nodded as if she understood.

"You best get to bed, little man."

Israel walked out into the steaming night. Crickets chirped, and bats whirred overhead, erratic in their flight. Why didn't I tell her about the devil man? he wondered. It would've just worried her. And besides…Mr. King couldn't be the Devil, could he? His elixir had gone down both his and Tansy's throat as smooth as silk. It had been firewater to Master Rufus. But he still had the stench of witchery and hoodoo about him. Israel reached the shack that he shared with Old Mark. Mark was in bed, and woke up when Israel entered. He gestured toward the stove with his hand. A faint, glottal crackle sounded from his mouth—words strangled by spit and the stump of a tongue.

In the belly of the stove, Israel found a tin plate of pigs' feet, a thick slice of bread, a few chunks of sweet potato and collards.

"Thank you."

Mark coughed in acknowledgement. Israel banked the embers, and began eating the food, using the bread slice as an edible spoon.

After placing the empty dish with others waiting to be cleaned, he crawled into bed beside Old Mark.

Behind his closed eyes, he saw laughing green eyes.

If he thought that there would be a visible change in himself, after last night, Israel was sadly mistaken. The day began as sullenly as any. A cock crowed, a dawn as red as a wattle, and Ebbitt's morning work song threaded through the slave shacks. By the time he and Old Mark had splashed water on their faces from the pump, the insistent sizzle of cicadas began. A fine sweat broke out on both their faces, as they left to their separate tasks, Old Mark in the tobacco fields, Izzy to the big house.

He was, for now at least, a kitchen boy. The Summer Kitchen was a hot, close cave presided over with gleeful industry by Gilbert, also known as Giggles, for his frequent, nervous laughter.

Giggles could have been the King of Hell—Izzy couldn't imagine Hell being any hotter than here. It was still early morning, and already the men and women of the Summer Kitchen were soaked through with sweat from the roaring fires and bubbling pots. It beaded brows and formed irregular stains on linens. A few men, shirtless and glistening, rolled a barrel of something or other. The floor was already littered with peelings and the skins of onions. One of Moonflower's many nameless cats played with the discarded potato sprout on the grimy floor. The cat's coat sagged, its ears drooped. Giggles, on the other hand, was immune. His outfit, starched stiff and white, betrayed nary a fleck of moisture. His dark skin was shiny, but not slick.

Presently, he was supervising one of the ladies in preparation of greens. "Now, you just warna put a little hot pepper in that there pot liquor. Miz Jones, she don't like it too hot. A zap or two will help her constitution, ha ha!"

When the woman was left alone with the greens, Giggles turned and surveyed his domain. His great black face split in a friendly smile at Israel. "Boy, you come here. I want you to get some cream from outta one of them prize heifers. I'm making a fancy French dessert, a blank mange, and I need a whole lotta cream."

While Israel didn't look forward to hauling buckets of milk, at least he'd be free from the sweltering kitchen. The barn was about a quarter of mile away from the Summer Kitchen. Dark and close, smelling of sweet hay cut by sharp manure, it was hot but still a million degrees cooler. Flies frenzied over hidden piles of shit and the asses of the animals. Each lazy flick of a tail set another flurry in motion. Israel walked past stall after stall, until he found the one with Cristabel in it.

"'bel," said Israel softly; he didn't want to startle her too much. "'bel, I need some cream."

She opened her eyes. Even in the shadowed barn, they were lambent. A startling, impossible blue. The stall she'd found had a draft of some kind. It was cool, like the floor of a cave.

She nodded, and began playing the pink udders of the cow in front of her like a peculiar instrument. The hissing and frothing sounds she made were hypnotic. In the hot stillness, he could almost doze as well.

When the bucket was full, she skimmed the cream off the top, and put it in another bucket. She did this three times, to three indifferent cows. When she was done, he had a half full bucket.

"That all you need?" It was the first time she'd spoken to him. This wasn't surprising; Cristabel was known for her moods. She was from one of the islands, and had a faint lilt to her accent, when she bothered to speak at all.

"Should do for now." She nodded, and vanished into her small grotto, with one of the smaller cows and a stool.

This wasn't so bad. Just two buckets, one cream, the other milk. He carried the buckets to the front of barn. Before he reached the line where dark ground became illuminated, he heard Cristabel speak.

"'Bel? 'Bel, did you say something?" He paused.

When he heard nothing, he started again toward the light, thinking of the quarter of a mile in the hot sun. It was cool here, underneath the roof. Chinks of brightness penetrated the roof, but mostly it was dark. Black and greenish-black, like an algae glutted pond.

"I said, it's like you never wanna leave." Cristabel's voice. He turned slightly. She was peeking out of her little hidey-hole, sleepily. Her eyes flashed in the dark, before she went into her stall. Blue, green, blue.

When he arrived, with aching arms and sweating body, to the Summer Kitchen, Giggles gave him yet another task. A pound of sugar from the pantry; climb up the ladder and get a few onions. By noon, he was exhausted. Heat had no effect on him.

That afternoon brought the boring task of setting the table. It went smoothly, until he broke a gravy boat up too high to reach easy. It lay in pieces on the floor. One of the maids swept it up without a word. Israel believed that the Joneses had thousands of the things. The dish closet was the size of his cabin. Candlesticks, silver and linens were laid on the table.

A quick break for dinner—scraps of chicken, corn pone, a cup of buttermilk—and then the final preparations. Candles lit, dishes laid on the sideboard, a cavalry of maids hovering around the edges of the halo that encompassed the family. Tansy was one of these maids.

Master Jones arrived first. Not surprising. He was a rotund man, whose beet-red face was framed by thick tufted muttonchops. Mrs. Jones came next, supported by Harte, the porter. She was like a frail doll engulfed by her hoop skirt. Like Bertha, she wore a shawl, though it was sweltering inside. The children—two girls, a year apart, but dressed in matching striped green dresses, bows and pinafores, entered, with wild Master Rufus following. He gave Israel a clandestine scowl before taking his seat. Mrs. Jones led the house in a prayer as solemn and homely as the samplers she incessantly sewed. Dishes were carried to the table, Tansy with sugar snap green peas, another maid with a roasted chicken scented with rosemary, thyme and onion. Israel scuttled around, making sure that water and wine glasses were filled. Discussion centered on the tobacco fields, and upcoming parties. It was apparent that Master Rufus was bored out of his mind.

"And what did Mr. Snicket teach you, son?" Mrs. Jones inquired.

"Dunno. Greek mythology, I suppose." He rattled off his answers.

"Son, don't slouch. And answer your mother in full sentences."

The almost-twins snickered.

Dinner ended with Giggles' blank mange and glasses of port for the adults. The young ladies were led off to bed, soon followed by their parents. Master Rufus sat at the table, swirling his port.

"Israel, come here."

Israel put down the dirty dish he was carrying to the kitchen on the sideboard. "Yes, sir."

"Have a seat, boy."

He chanced a glance at Master Rufus. Pale, freckled, an unruly mop of reddish-brown hair, there was something clownish about him to make him too menacing. "No, sir. Ain't right I should be sitting with my superiors." He looked down at his scuffed shoes instead.

"Have it your way. But I want you to look at me."

Israel looked up into limpid pools of malt-brown. They held his image and a candle flame.

"I want to tell me the truth. Where'd you get that nasty moonshine?"

He was about to say from Cletus. The words almost fell from his lips. But the image of the ghostly black man would not leave his mind. A breath escaped from between his lips. He didn't answer.

Quick as a snake, Master Rufus snatched his wrists, and squeezed them, constricting the blood. "You don't wanna talk, that's fine with me." His white face came real close to his. Israel smelled the port on his breath. "Just don't ever do that again, you hear me? If you do, so help me, I'll beat the black right off of your ass." His wrists were bracelets of pain, but Israel didn't whimper. That would make it worse.

After an especially hard squeeze, Rufus released him. Israel resisted the urge to rub his sore wrists. They were probably purple, beneath his shirt.

Rufus smiled. Clown-like again. "We're still friends, though. Can't be mad at you." He chuckled, and ruffled the top of Israel's head. "I know you did that, that joke, cuz you're in love with Tansy. I'll tell you what," Rufus leaned forward, like he was conspiring, "you play your cards right, one of these days you might get Tansy. I'll make sure you'll have her."

He drained his port, and stumbled off into the rest of manse.

Israel didn't have time to collect his thoughts about the scene. Tansy appeared, and whisked him into the kitchen. "What did that bastard do to you?"

"It ain't nothing."

She didn't even listen to him. She pulled back the sleeves of his shirt, and clucked concern.

"Giggles," she yelled. "Come here and give me one of your poultices for burns."

"Somebody got burned, did they, ha ha! Izzy didn't scorch himself on the candle again, did he?"

Tansy was resolute. "The poultice."

A few minutes later, an evil-smelling, greasy brown concoction was slathered over his wrists. "You still hurt?"

It was tempting to say yes. He'd probably get to sleep in her bed that night. "Naw. Ain't nothing. I got to help clean up—"

"No, you don't. Just sit on this stool. It'll be taken care of. I'll walk you back to Old Mark's."

Tansy flounced out of the winter kitchen, into the dining room. She returned with the remains of the blank mange and set it in front of Israel.

"Here, eat this."

"That's okay."

"I said, eat this. Or I'll make you eat it." She smiled as she handed him a spoon.

When she went back into the dining room, Israel poked at the ethereal custard. It quivered. It was milk jelly. The first bite went down smooth. He'd never tasted anything so light and sweet. Sugar and vanilla mingled in his mouth. It tasted like breast milk, or at least what he thought breast milk should taste like. But that was silly. As if he'd even had a mother.

A half hour later, Tansy took him back from the manse to the slave shacks.

"What did he do that for, Izzy? Why was he bothering you?" She'd stopped him, just before the first of the shacks appeared.

"Dunno. The moonshine, probably."

"Uh." They started walking again. "Has no business drinking moonshine in the first place. Listen to me." She stopped again. "If I even hear of him doing something like that, I will personally—I don't know what I'd do."

Her eyes flashed in the dark. Some trick of the moonlight gave them a green cast. He'd never seen her so angry.

A few more minutes in silence, and they were closer to his and Old Mark's cabin. Bertha and Tansy's was a couple of feet away. Rufus stepped out of the front door of that shack.

"Hey, gal," he said, slow and easy.

Tansy's face was tight. He could feel the dread coming off her in waves. A killing urge welled up in him, hotter than the night, sharper than the sounds of the crickets and cicadas.

"We can't," she said. She moved towards her door, gripping Israel's arms. "First, it's my time of the month. 'Sides, someone's gotta take care of this child."

Rufus chuckled, a bit of smoke escaping his nostrils. Izzy could see the low ember of the mule shit cigarette burning in the night. "I don't believe you," he drawled. "And the boy's just fine."

"What don't you believe?" Tansy raised her voice. "You can look at my bleeding hole yourself, if you want." She hitched up her skirt.

"Stop that!" Rufus dropped the cigarette in surprise. A red flake drifted to the ground. "And keep your voice down— "

"'The boy is fine,'? How would you know? Did you take care him afterwards? No, you just went up to your room to smoke."

"Don't you talk to me like that!" He walked right up to her. "You're on thin ice, bitch."

She faced him. "So are you. Beating a little boy. Drinking moonshine. Fucking a nigger bitch. I'm sure that your papa would just love to hear that."

Rufus swiped at her but she moved out of his reach. "Keep it down," he growled.

"Why do I got to keep it down? It's not like the people here don't know what's going on." Tansy lowered her voice, the green cast in her eye strong. "If you want to keep things private, you best listen to me. I'll take your cracker-cock. But don't you ever lay a hand on this child, or any other child again."

He punched her then. Hard, right in the stomach.

Tansy didn't even blink. She held her ground. This enraged Rufus even more, and he punched her face. Israel closed his eyes. Surely, her face was a ruin of blood and bone. Israel heard another crack against her, and readied to hurl himself at Rufus.

But Tansy stood tall. Her face was unmarked. Frustrated, Rufus began to choke her, bruising her neck with his fat, grub-pale fingers. Instead she laughed a wicked sound, one that drew out an audience.

"That the best you can do?" she said. With grace and nonchalance, she pushed him away. A tap on his chest, and his grip on her neck released. Rufus ended up on the ground, looking foolish.

Tansy took Israel's hand, and they stepped over Rufus's prostrate body, a quivering blank mange that whimpered. Low and dangerous, Tansy said, "Just think about what I could do if I put my mind to it." And she closed the door to her shack.

The shutting of the door was an ending. Dangerous Tansy evaporated like dew. The fury on what should have been her ruined face relaxed; the tension on her should-have-been bruised neck unknotted.

"You okay?"

Israel nodded in agreement.

"You want something to drink? No? Then wash up, and come to bed."

While Tansy set about lighting the kerosene lamps, Israel walked past the dozing Bertha to the basin, and splashed water on his face. *What the Hell did I just see?* Tansy was meek and sweet. Naïve and God-fearing, as a Negro woman ought to be, probably why Rufus picked her to fuck in the first place. The change of nature was freakish, like a plague of frogs or snow in April. What if it was that moonshine from the man under the briars? She did take a mighty long sip of it. Israel shivered. Excitement threaded its way up and down his spine. A warmth in the belly.

"Izzy, what you tarrying for? Come to bed."

She was preternaturally calm, for a woman who had cussed out the Master's son, and hit him to boot. As if it hadn't happened. Israel's glee at seeing Rufus laid flat on his backside was interrupted by sudden fear. There'd be punishment? Images of past torchlit punishments came into his mind. The lash of the whip.

They couldn't trust Rufus not to tell. He was craven; what would stop?

Israel crawled into bed, and Tansy extinguished the kerosene lamp. She wished him goodnight, and kissed him. He waited until he heard her breathing easy, then a few minutes 'til his eyes had adjusted to the dark.

'L'il cat,' Rufus had said. Israel shuddered. He crept out of bed on all fours, and crawled until he reached the corner of the cabin. The elegant bottle of moonshine easy to find. It glowed with green moonlight. Israel uncapped it, and took a long swig. Honeysuckle, wild roses, deep ponds all went down his throat. He could taste guitar notes, and voices raised in song. All the aspects of green, from earth to sky, went down into his belly, settled there, took root. He recapped the bottle, and crawled back to bed.

That should protect both of us. She'd only had half as much. He closed his eyes.

Green was everywhere, in all hues and saturations. Emerald, chartreuse, and lime. It came muted, with silver or blue or yellow. It floated above him, in leaves or eyes, in every shape imaginable. The green oozed warmth, promised coolness, dribbled and dripped from every surface. It was dizzying, and disorienting. The smell of freshness, cut grass, or pine needles, invaded him, coating the back of his throat. It was too much…

But slowly, the green focused, gem sharp, and Israel saw the green forming into discernable shapes. He was in a clearing of some kind; surrounded by thousands of trees, or branches… it was unclear, still. Green gave rise to other colors, black and brown (but they still had green in them). A chair, a table, a fireplace. But even those were not what they seemed. The chair, for instance, was a stump, its back a still-living sheath of wood. The table was a log, petrified, with patterns whorled on it. Only the hearth looked normal. A pot of something delicious bubbled away on greenish flames.

Israel looked up, and saw that the sky itself was green. Light, filtered through hundreds of leaves. The light was guarded by millions of fangs that sprouted from the elegant green and brown serpentine vines.

He gasped, "Where am I?"

Movement, out of the corner of his eye. A sleek brown and white shape streaked in the deeper part of the—forest? Whiskers, a round tail. A rabbit. A cough came to his left. Israel turned in that direction. Red and velvet, a fox stepped out of the thicket, into the clearing. It gave another coughing bark, and strode up to him. It sat down on its haunches, like a dog, and cocked its head, as if waiting for him to scratch between its ears.

"Don't mind him, he spoiled." The musky and sweet voice came from behind. He turned around and saw a bare breasted woman garbed in a loose skirt that was white; therefore, it was tinged with the palest green. The color of the bottle of liquor. Her breasts jutted out, large and brown, tipped by tender buds as black as night. He tried not to stare at their hypnotic symmetry. Her hair was wild, a swamp of twisted black braids. She had no face. She had a nose, eyes, and lips—all beautiful—but they wouldn't stay still. Her face rippled, supplanted by another, even more gorgeous facial features. She glided (or floated, he couldn't be sure, cause he didn't see feet) over to the cauldron on the fire before he could get a real good look. It seemed as if she swam the clearing.

Israel absently stroked the space between the fox's pointed ears. The fur was soft; it felt good to rub the inverted bowl of its head. The fox's eyes closed in pleasure.

He found his voice, "Who are you?"

She turned her disturbing face to him. He focused on her less disturbing perfect breasts.

There was amusement in her reply, "My name is…" Then came a spiral of phonetics, firm consonants and liquid vowels, slipped by him, redolent of musk, rustling leaves and sighing seas, all impossible to grasp. "But you may call me Mrs. King."

Ah, so he was underneath, within the briar patch, miles below the surface of the earth, imprisoned by thorns. This made sense.

"Where's Mr. King?"

Mrs. King turned back to the pot of bubbling stuff. Israel was thankful. He found it hard to look at her face, and hard not to look at her breasts.

"He's with Tansy." There was a jealous note in her voice. No, sadder than that.

"What…" Israel stopped. It made sense, sort of. By drinking the moonshine, he'd been asking for the Devil's—or Mr. King's—protection. He'd thought that he would be made stronger, like Tansy had been. But maybe it didn't work that way with everyone.

The fox grew bored of his attentions, and sulked off towards the greener gloom. Mrs. King turned to him, with a bowl of steaming stew in hand. She floated/glided over, and sat on a bench across from him. "Sitting" wasn't an accurate description. Even seated, the ends of her white skirt fluttered in an unseen tide.

She handed him the bowl along with a spoon. The aroma was wonderful. Earthy mushrooms and chunks of carrot floated atop of a rich brown broth. Israel's stomach growled. But something stopped him from digging right in.

Mrs. King smiled. "Go ahead and eat. Nothing is gonna hurt you."

He took a cautious bite of something soft and starchy—a sweet potato. He ate a few minutes in silence, just enjoying the sensation of knowing that there would be more food. By doing so, he wouldn't have to look at her shifting face(s).

When he was finished, he felt her hot green eyes on him. He took a breath, and looked directly at the blurring features of her face.

"Thank you, Mrs. King." She gave the barest nod. "It was delicious."

She waited expectantly. In spite of her constant motion, she seemed the essence of patience and calm.

"I have a question. I just—Who… what are you? You and your… husband?"

The words hung in the glade of green, thick fog on water. Mrs. King fluttered upward, and hovered towards the cauldron. She reached into one of the curling vines, and produced a pitcher. She scooped dirt from the ground, and threw it upon the fire, dousing the flames. Israel stood up with his dish, which was a kind of stone worn smooth, and walked toward her. She remained in front of the cauldron. When he reached her, he tapped her back, to let her know that he was behind her. She spun about, more quickly than he imagined, startling him. He dropped his dish. Stone and spoon fell with a sound absorbed by the earth.

"Who are we, you ask?" Tears moved down her awful, fractured face it, like rain down the facets of a diamond. "We, my husband and I, we are failures." She burned in green flame. "We are kings with no subjects. Warriors with no spears. Remnants, fragments—useless."

Israel stepped backwards. Her thick hair climbed some unknown breeze.

"Protectors and guides we once were. Now, we are helpless. Hopeless. We are no longer able to protect and nurture our children." She held her breasts, shimmering basalt, with her hands. "These ache with unused milk, until they wither, like dugs." Before his eyes, the firm dark plums became long and leathery. Her face resolved, into skin of brown, hard earth, cracked with sun and pain. The black roots of her hair frayed, became wire. It was white (and therefore, green).

It was the saddest thing he ever saw. Israel stretched his arms wide and reached for her. She reminded him of Bertha. She enfolded him. Her breasts, against his cheek, were soft and supple. He pressed his face against them, drinking in their smells. There was the tang of woman-sweat, and a salty sting. There was softness here, the velvet of Moonflower's curtains. He leaned a little back, and took one of the dark nipples into his mouth. It was cool and hard to the touch. Her hand pressed on the back of his head. He began to suck. A stream of honeysuckle milk poured into his mouth.

This, then, was the source of Mr. King's elixir. Israel tasted the summer days, Tansy's strength, guitar notes, jungles and myths. But underneath came the aftertaste of bitterness, confinement, the ocean's salt, the whip's sting. Even though there were these weird, unpleasant tastes, Israel longed to drink more. So he drank more. Her milk coated his throat and went down into his belly, curled there, and went to sleep.

A faint warmth, the tickle of green. He smelled her sweat, and heard her heartbeat. It was slow and deep, like an underground bell. He stopped sucking, and rested his head against her breasts. They were slick, and wet. A sour, coppery smell was in his nose. He was warm, enfolded in her arms. Warm. Too warm. The bell rang slower, the moments between its sounding stretching and stretching. Fingernails (or thorns) snagged into his arm. And she was no longer cradling his head.

"Mrs. King," he said. Israel opened his eyes. There wasn't no green light anywhere. And her breasts—they wasn't bare. A thin sheet of cotton separated him from them. He wasn't standing but lying down.

He pulled himself away, and upright. A few strays of weak light slipped through the chinks in a wall. He realized he was in Tansy's cabin, and, Tansy lying in a tangled heap on the bed.

A stream of blood came from her mouth, which was bruised, dark and slightly open. Blood-slicked teeth caught what little light there was in the room, and reflected it. Her eyes, though closed, were swollen, seething with dark blood. Her nose was crushed, and he could see the tattoo of bruising along her neck. Her chest didn't rise. She was still.

The green and new of summer had left her. She was a husk, a form, now discarded.

Israel remembered the stillness. It lasted a long time, maybe forever. But eventually, that shallow pool quiet was shattered.

The scream was like a pebble, thrown into a stagnant pool. The ripples began slowly, gradually building momentum, until waves crashed against a shore.

In the end, they found the three of them. The dead girl. The frozen boy. The wailing mother.

The rest of the slaves buried Tansy in the evening, at twilight. There was a burial ground for just such a purpose behind the slave shacks. Little wooden crosses poked out of the ground in neatly contained rows. The town reverend had been invited to say a few meaningless words, about what a docile woman Tansy Jones was, along with various psalms and lessons from the Bible about good servants. He assured the masses that Tansy—officially dead from a sudden fever—wandered the hills and valleys of Heaven, garbed in white, with wings, at the feet of the Lord.

Mrs. Jones was there, looking gaunt, along with the almost-twin girls. All three wore black. The girls wriggled and snickered, while Mrs. Jones did her best to look mournful. To the melodious lowing of a spiritual, Tansy's plain wooden casket was lowered into the earth, quickly followed by clods of dirt.

Israel was with Bertha, mostly numb. When his turn came, he tossed the dirt into the yawning hole without looking. Bertha tightly clutched the patch of earth in her hand when it was handed to her, as if it were a treasure. Israel made a feeble attempt to wrest it from her hands, but gave up.

Mrs. Jones and her daughters walked up to Bertha, hoop skirts sweeping the crumbs of dirt. Her daughters were nearly skipping, and whispering to one another. A dark glance from their mother silenced them—momentarily.

"Your daughter was an angel," Mrs. Jones said, gently touching Bertha's shoulder. Bertha just stared at the white woman; she could have been a gnat. "She shall be missed. But the Creator has other plans for her."

There was still no response.

One of the almost-twins fidgeted. "Marmee," she trilled, "why doesn't she speak?"

The other girl, apparently the younger, said, "She looks like she's dead."

Mrs. Jones swatted at her brood, which they swiftly sidestepped. "Children! It isn't polite to speak in front of people like that. Bertha is mourning."

Meanwhile, Israel boiled inside. To those girls, Tansy's funeral was like a trip to the market or a visit to Charlestown. A chance to wear a different costume. And Mrs. Jones continued the fake story of Tansy's death. Before he knew it, he was yelling at them. He didn't care what happened to him. "She's deaf." Mrs. Jones spared him a glance. "Bertha is deaf. You'd know that, if you cared. And Tansy didn't die of no fever."

The choir stopped singing. There was silence all around. All eyes were on him.

The older 'twin' broke the tension. "You aren't supposed to talk like that. Nig—Darkies are only to speak when spoken to." She said with the smugness of a nursery rhyme.

"Susannah, that's rude," Mrs. Jones said absently. "Israel, what do you mean, Tansy didn't die of fever?"

Israel held her weak gaze in his own—and lost courage. *Ask Rufus*, he wanted to say. But he didn't. Instead, he broke free of funeral party, leaving both Mrs. Jones and Bertha bewildered. He ran.

The briar patch wasn't any less sinister. The thorns glittered in the dying sunlight. Cobwebs covered some of them, like gossamer. Flies lazily hovered above the treacherous expanse.

"Where are you?" Israel screamed. There was no response. "Why did you let them kill her?"

He imagined the old man in his hammock under the sea of thorns, waking up. *What he yelling about?* he would say to his shifty wife.

Don't you worry none about it, the wife of a thousand faces would reply.

They were wicked, the Devil and his wife. They'd tricked him. Israel's rage spilled over. He wanted to rip apart the thorns, until he came upon their green haven. He would knock over Mrs. King's pot, and set fire to the whole damn place, guitar, fox and all. Another part of him wanted to jump down into the thorns, and let them take him to where Tansy was. Pain would be a small price to pay to visit her. The rivers of milk, the lakes of honey—he didn't care for any of that. Just her kindness. Her near him. But he wasn't worth it. He could never be near her. Just when he'd had the chance, he'd chickened out.

"...over here..."

Israel glanced up, to see a procession of other slaves, led by Isabel. They were coming to take him away. He didn't know why, but Izzy felt it was his last chance to do something. The canyon of thorns awaited him with their cruelty. Fangs beckoned him. They blurred. It would be so easy to greet them. Maybe they wouldn't bite him. Maybe it was an illusion. They were as tender and safe as Tansy's arms….

"…what…"

"Stop him!"

"Izzy, don't, chile!"

Arms—they wasn't Tansy's—lifted him up. He struck at them. He shrieked, "Let me go! Lemme go." A forest of arms (unthorned) held him against his will. "He killed her! He killed her." And a thousand voices (not as many as there were shifting faces) told him to calm down. It was alright. They knew. "I need her, I want to go to her." Child, you can't. The Lord will call you when the time is right. "No, not the Lord. I don't want to see him…" His voice died. And he could see. Melting glass blocked his view. In twilight they took him from the safe place. Where thorns were velvet, guitars had eyes, and liquor tasted like mother's milk.

He was swimming toward them. Devils or angels? He didn't care.

When he woke up, Israel found himself in bed. Someone was wiping his brow. He could smell her, hay and sweat. Startling blue eyes gazed down at him, framed in a black face. Cristabel.

Israel stared at her in an easy silence that seemed to last for a long time. He acclimated himself to waking. He could tell, from the slant of the light, that it was late afternoon. Birds chattered amongst themselves, and crickets began their tentative chirping. He must have slept, for most of a day. Then, memory hit him like a wave. Tansy was dead. And he was still alive.

Cristabel interrupted his slide into despair. "You sleep a long time," she said.

He turned away. He didn't want to hear her.

"You hungry? I guess you not." She dropped the dishrag in basin, and sat down next to him. Israel closed his eyes. He didn't want to feel anything.

When he surfaced again from the clutch of sleep, it was even darker. A couple kerosene lamps were lit, and he could hear Mark near the stove, probably heating up the mush they served the workers. Israel sat up, and saw Cristabel dozing next to him. Some knitting that she'd been working lay sprawled out in front of her. In the half-light provided by the lamps, Israel saw it was a quilt. Within its folds he could make out shapes of branches, densely clustered together, held together by leaves, thistles and thorns—

"Cristabel. 'Bel."

The woman snorted awake. Her eyes shone, gaining focus. "Now he wants to eat," she said. "Just when I comfortable."

Mark coughed in mock sympathy.

Israel didn't want to eat, but he endured Mark and Cristabel's nurturing. They gave him half of Mark's cornmeal and fat-studded mush, and a cup of warm tea, sweetened with sorghum. He ate obligingly, without hunger. After they were sure he'd eaten enough— Cristabel hovering like a bee, Mark sputtering and gasping like a clogged bellows—Israel got Cristabel's attention.

"Your quilt."

She grabbed at it. "What 'bout it?"

"Let me see it."

She handed it to him. It was a woven briar patch, littered with eyes and faces. Here and there, animals were captured in the morass. A rabbit skittered gaily through the thorns. A raccoon scrambled above the vines, unpierced. Was that a leaf—or an eye? Or a hand— of ivy, or flesh? The artwork, of felt scraps, pieces of curtain, old work dungarees, a discarded dress pattern, was crude and childish. Yet, it lived. It moved and surged. The briar patch of fabric moved and slithered. Felt and fabric wove and unwove. That purple squirrel, this gingham cat surged and merged. The quilt was edged with a pattern of green flowers against white, the remains of an old flour sack. Stitches crisscrossed and mesmerized. Thorns became knitting needles. A fly of felt rose from the quilted briar. The green flowers glowed and released the odor of lanolin, mixed with sulfur.

When Israel looked up from the surging quilt, he wasn't surprised to see the green glint coming out of both Cristabel and Mark's eyes.

Cristabel spoke first, in a voice that was both hers and *hers*. (A thousand shifting faces. Why not a thousand shifting voices?). "Don't hate us, Israel." Sap-like tears rolled down Cristabel's face.

"I tried my best," said Mark, or Mr. King. His voice was a cough and dark, secret places. "But we are weak."

Mrs. King nodded. "We're fading."

Israel sighed, crumbling the quilt. "You can't do anything. You're worse than the Devil."

Mr. King had the guitar in his hand. It shimmered into existence. Mrs. King sat back in her chair, cradling a felt fox. Mr. King began playing the guitar. It was soothing and warm, like heated syrup. Israel's eyes became heavier. The song of summer, honeysuckle and red clay sent him spiraling towards the haven of sleep. The quilt still moved, and promised the safety of thorns.

Israel forced himself awake, and broke the spell.

"Y'all are weak and fading," he told the ghostly couple. "But I ain't."

Etiolate

Oliver stood in the crowd, a part of its number, yet apart from its essence. They were smoking, high, garbed in black, whorled with tattoos, pierced with silver hoops. They smelled of cloves, cK1, and leather. They were pale, perhaps dusted here with pink, a hint of a blue vein there, in sudden relief against their flesh.

They were pale; he was dark. Dark skin, with black wool for hair that was darker than the clothing they wore. He was out of place: black sheep.

"See that guy over there?" His friend Pompeii had returned, carrying some Creme de Menthe concoction contrived to look like absinthe. "Isn't *she* cute?" Pompeii's voice was fey and sickly sweet. He dressed in his club-kid gear: silver booty shorts, mesh tee shirt and combat boots.

Oliver looked over the crowd.

"Not at all. He's so eighties. Feathered, bleached hair, black ruffles on his shirt, those ankle boots... That scene is so tired. A spectacle of sadness on parade. He's like Robert Smith and Peter Murphy all rolled into one."

"Sweetcakes, I was talking about *her*."

"She" was a boy dressed in black and electric blue lycra, with platform sneakers. Oliver rolled his eyes. "No. I'm afraid I don't think…" But then, Pompeii would never understand. He was a post-rave boy-slut who still used his name from his Goth days. Oliver had given his up long ago. It had been Zothique, after an obscure author's fantasy world. Like his friend's moniker, it was a doomed and lost society, full of magic and decadence. Now the whole thing left him empty.

Oliver took a swig of beer. It was warm. He could taste the barley.

"You don't like that type anymore, honey?"

There was implication in the statement, as innocent as it was.

He considered Pompeii, with his exotic beauty. He was Persian, and his real name was Duncan. His turmeric skin, liquid brown eyes and black hair still bewitched him. Yes. Pompeii had beauty that he did not. Pompeii was one of them.

A few minutes later, Pompeii took to the dance floor. Months ago, he would have followed, if only to be closer to that sea of gyrating flesh. He was left with his warm beer. He stopped nursing it.

The Gotham was a shadow of its former glory. The grimy black club no longer held any glamour. Mannequin heads were draped with veils and twinkling Christmas lights. The tables had faded stencils of snowflakes and doilies on them. And a thousand TV monitors flashed underground videos and scenes from cult movies. He caught a glimpse of Patty Duke in *The Valley of the Dolls*, held captive in a bathtub. Her face was pale with blue veins showing through, and she was mouthing "Give me my dolls!" Months ago he would have laughed at that scene, while popping "dolls" of his own—E, and crystal meth. The surging crowds of young people, who wanted to be *Blade Runner* extras, or vampires, were no longer his family. They never were.

Bauhaus throbbed on the stereo system. A girl in a fairy-tale lace blouse and black rubber pants winked at him from across the room.

He knew that this was not a sexual come-on; most people assumed he was queer, even though he wasn't pretty. It was an offer for drugs. He'd bought from her before. He moved towards the stage.

Within ten minutes, the lights went down, and the band Ganesa took the stage. The scene left him hollow, but its soundtrack transcended. With her trademark sari, the coffee-dark singer wailed out ghazals, muezzin's cries, and torch-song lyrics against swirling electronic music punctuated by drum machine beats. At one point during the show, she plucked a sitar, during a new song called "Kali". When he closed his eyes, Oliver could see a land of tigers, monkeys, scented with jasmine and curry. Her smoky voice and the twang of the sitar drifted on veils of synths and discreet tablas. Opening his eyes after the song, Oliver saw the black-clad tribe, winding down from the faux-Egyptian dances. When "Ivory" started, he once again closed his eyes. He knew that he was missing out on the singer's movements, but the callowness of the crowd was getting to him. The song's verses switched from English to Hindi. During one particularly intense moment, someone bumped into him. A boot grazed his foot.

"Would you…" He didn't finish the sentence.

"Why don't you watch where you're going, dude?"

The boy who'd bumped into him was perfect. Thin as a stalk of grass with wheat-gold hair and blue eyes. The black of his clothing was sensible, elegant even; it heightened the white of his flesh. He was young, a waif. The fullness of his lips was reminiscent of models used in the Calvin Klein kiddie-porn campaign. His scrawny body had a used look, and there was a suburban feral glint in his eyes. He wore a Nine-Inch-Nails T-shirt. Through his hurt, Oliver wanted him. The boy gave him a glance, then looked away.

Did he expect anything else? He closed his eyes, giving himself to the music. Here was the sensuality and the mystery of sex. A bit too abstract, but it would have to do.

To the trance-like beat of the music, Oliver could imagine being with the boy. His dorm room, sepia with the light of the city, salty and sooty with the attack of Baltimore's air. Something mellow, and fuzzy would be playing—"My Bloody Valentine," perhaps. A few nervous giggles; then the boy (he looked like a Brian) would take out a nickel bag of crushed brown leaves. "No thanks; I don't need—" "OK," Brian would stuff the bag back into his jacket. "I don't need that, when I have you," or some such crap like that. And he would kiss him, his ice and hash, his breath mint-sweet and beer-sour. The first gentle moments, fingers circling a nipple, erecting it. The thrill of hands on flesh (pale on dark). "I've never been with a black man." Breaths mingling, then lips. Then the clumsy, graceful removal of clothes, groins grinding against each other, fingers digging for bone, fingers crumbling dirt.

Oliver grew hard. He could feel it straining against his trousers. The back of his neck was cool, with a slight moisture. Like someone had been breathing on it.

He opened his eyes, and spun around.

The breather wore a Coil T-shirt tight against his well-defined body. The I's dot was in the center of a nipple, the right one. There was the indentation of a ring on the left one. The slacks were black, and immaculate. More than black—they had a supernatural blue sheen to them, like the coats of seals in moonlight. The shoes, not quite Doc Martens, were adorably scuffed. The breather's skin was white. His hair was silver. His eyes hid behind dark, Italian movie star glasses. He smiled at Oliver.

His jaw must have dropped; the guy laughed, and moved closer.

"Hey," he said, "I'm—" and his name was lost, in music, in crowd, in the noise of his racing pulse.

"Listen, Oliver—cool name, by the way—we should talk. After the show." And he turned toward the stage.

Oliver nodded. When he turned to the stage, a pair of hands rested lightly on his shoulders. The rest of Ganesa's set, only the hands—of ice, or marble, yet warm—existed. He could feel bone, the slightest whisper of blood, the texture of skin through the shirt.

What was the breather's (what was his name?) favorite Coil album? What was beneath the Coil shirt?

For once, he wished the band would hurry and finish. The final Ganesa song was a wordless acapella piece. Her voice soared. Oliver's heart raced; what he felt for—Silver—was beyond words, too. The lights dimmed; a puff of smoke obscured the band members, except for the glow of the singer's bindi. The smoke smelled of coconut. The hands on his shoulder let go. Oliver turned around slowly (he didn't want to seem too eager).

Silver smiled. Before Oliver could say a word, he said, "Let's meet outside, where we can talk." He began pushing through the crowd. Oliver stood still, reeling. Did that just happen? *A beautiful guy wants me?*

Pompeii interrupted his anxiety. "You OK? You look bothered. What was his name, sweetie?"

"I don't know."

"That bad? Well, this is Cameron." Pompeii paraded his new trick (cute, young, impeccably dressed) before him, "and we're going home together. You gonna be okay?"

"Yeah…" *What will I talk to him about? I'll talk about Coil, and see who else he likes. Maybe he can come home and watch that Jarman movie. And then—* "Oh, Pompeii. His number. Just in case."

His friend turned, and asked his new toy to write his phone number down. "I don't know why he wants me to; there's really no danger. I mean, if you piss me off, darling, I'll rip you to shreds, cause I'm a real bitch. A velociraptor-bitch." This was all said with a smile. When Cameron was finished, Pompeii handed the scrap of paper to Oliver, and kissed him goodnight. The two went out of the club.

Oliver followed behind them a few seconds later.

The night was hazy; a jaundiced mist smeared over everything. In the distance, the factories belched smoke, and tall antennae blinked red dots, like floating bindis. The smell of Baltimore—fish, rubber, sweat—filled Oliver's nostrils. The mica in the street sparkled underneath street lamps, corrupted flecks of silver. He emerged from a billow of the disgusting haze.

"I was about to go," he said, sauntering up to him.

"I'm sorry; my friend… he was going home with someone we didn't know, so I had to stay behind and make sure—"

"That's cool. You're a good friend, a real sweetie. Me, I'd say, fuck 'em. If I'm not getting any, I'm sure as hell not gonna help them with their success."

Oliver laughed; Silver smirked.

"By the way, I didn't catch your name. The pounding music and all."

"That's not true—you wasn't paying attention." The man pulled his jacket tight. "Let's walk about. Great weather; a bit H.P. Lovecraft, isn't it? Any minute, some Nameless, Faceless, Indescribable Horror is gonna jump out at you. But that's Baltimore for you: mixture of banality and evil. The banality of evil. Evil banality. Sounds like a great band name, doesn't it, Oliver? What kind of music would it be?"

"I dunno. Industrial, maybe."

"No. Wrong. I was envisioning a trio of scantily-clad women— one white, one black, one Asian—performing cookie-cutter pop music, written by, say, Babyface, or those guys who do Janet Jackson. It would be truth in advertising, at least."

They walked through a seedy area and passed by the cemetery where Poe was buried. They talked more. Oliver asked him about music. It seemed that Silver and he had similar tastes, though Silver was more adventurous. Coil, Cocteaus, Dead Can Dance, Aphex Twin, Current 93… And Silver rattled off names of bands he'd heard about, but never listened to.

"I'll have to come by and borrow some stuff."

"I know what else you'd like to 'borrow.'" He winked.

And Oliver felt good, for the first time in a long time. As they walked, he leaned into Silver; the man complied by putting his arm around his shoulder.

Adrenaline rushed, as did blood. The touch was soothing, cooling; it dispersed the haze. They made a full circuit, walking past the cemetery again, heading for the Gotham club. Silver was elusive and enigmatic to all of Oliver's prying:

"What do you do for a living?"

"How East Coast of you; back in SF, people would never ask that question. They recognized that a person has a life beyond their nine-to-five existence."

"So you're from California?"

"I didn't say that. But you are a Baltimore native, through and through; I know that much."

"How can you tell that?"

His tapped the side of his head. "Sixth sense."

They arrived in front of another club, where a few stragglers milled around.

"So we're here; and here is where the night ends," said Silver, and gave Oliver's shoulders a quick squeeze.

Oliver was disappointed; the night wasn't going to end with them curled together. "Well, let me have your number."

"No. Not yet."

"Why not?"

The albino did not answer immediately. He smiled, then said, "The mystery would be revealed too soon."

"I'll give you mine." Oliver reached in his coat for a pen.

"Don't bother. I'll get in contact with you, when I want to."

"But. Tell me your name, at least." He was being toyed with, but he didn't mind. Being toyed with was better than being ignored.

"You know it already," was all he said. "Now, I have to get going. We will see each other around, I promise. Don't look so despondent, now. I want you to be happy." Silver removed his glasses. His eyes were dark pink, with black centers, striated like the petals of a flower. The center of the flower held Oliver's image, black against black. He leaned forward; Silver kissed him lightly on the lips. Oliver closed his eyes, tasting menthol, florid perfume, and sweet tobacco. The silver contact was broken, the flower-eyes concealed. The man turned, and walked away, into haze, into mist, black sealskin pants, Celtic tattooed armbands, and golden letters on dark: *Love's Secret Domain*.

He left Oliver with a painful erection, and frustrated. *The fucker! He was just playing with me, and he's probably laughing to himself. Turned on a black faggot, something he wouldn't touch with a 10-foot pole.* The thought of his black flesh mingling with silver would only tarnish it.

When he was first came out—to himself—Oliver had been tormented by his feelings twofold: for men, and then for white men. The gay men he knew were obsessed with beauty—its Classical, Western definition. He was out. When eventually he found his way into the goth scene, that feeling of being a blemish was heightened. What was goth about, after all? The paleness of skin, black to accentuate the white, white pancake makeup to hide pigment. The wispy androgyny, the vague mysticism, and the harder, fascistic imagery were all aspects of the need for whiteness. They ignored him at first; then gradually tolerated him. But he was a campy Blacula to their elegant, aesthete vampires. He'd never slept with a goth, though it was an abiding desire of his. No, his tricks were over 40, men who though that he was street trash, who would bring jungle and jive and abandon to their beds. He often complied, and when he was tired of complying, he stopped. His need to couple with pale flesh would be overwhelmed by his disgust at the role he had to fulfill. "Fuck me, my little black slave-boy," was the refrain of one of his tricks. Yet, even now, as disgusting as that was, he would tolerate it. *Damn him for turning me on!* So close, and yet denied. *Why did I ever give up drugs?* When on E, it didn't matter. The crispy, fuzzy love you felt for your fellow human beings crossed boundaries, and horniness was obliterated.

Oliver closed his eyes, willing his erection away. He was determined not to have this night end with Harbor-side cruising, or in a smelly sex club. The sex clubs in DC were better; he briefly entertained going down there. But it was 50 miles away, and all of the clubs were in a bad neighborhood. *Just give up, Oliver. You'll never get what you need. Not now.* He opened his eyes, and walked towards his car.

"Hey, dude," a voice behind him said. He turned, and saw that first beautiful boy of the evening, the one who had stepped onto his foot. (And ignored him). "Do you think you could give me a ride? I don't live too far from here." He looked so young and pathetic; in another world, if Burton had made the third Batman movie, this kid would have been cast as Boy Wonder. He'd been so rude to him, before. But then, he was white and beautiful; it was his right to be rude to those who weren't.

"All right," Oliver said, "where do you live?"

"Thanks, dude! I live just north of Little Italy."

The car choked as it started. The streets—or the ghosts of streets—slipped by, drenched in jaundiced mist.

Boy Wonder chattered throughout the journey. "You like Ganesa? I think they're cool. This was my third time seeing them. Each time, they get better."

"Yeah. Were you at their other shows?"

"Yeah."

"I thought you look familiar. Didn't you used to have purple hair?"

"Uh-huh. I've outgrown it." Boy Wonder had noticed him before?

"I thought it was cool; you don't see many blacks—I mean, African-Americans, you know, listening to this music."

Oliver gave him a glance. Boy Wonder smiled slyly. His teeth were uneven. He was breathing slowly. And he'd taken off his shirt. Beneath the Nine-Inch-Nails shirt, the stigmata of his nipples glistened with sweat.

"What…"

"It's pretty hot and gross outside." His sunken chest heaved, slowly.

Oliver wasn't sure how it began, but he felt a tugging at his crotch. When he looked down, he saw a pale hand massaging him.

"You don't mind, do you, dude?"

"Not. At. All." Oliver pulled over, and placed his hand on the kid's crotch.

"Not here. I have a nice place…"

Two blocks later, down a sidewalk of mist like yellowed lace, and up some stairs (past a living room of stoned and ecstatic youths), they were writhing on a futon.

The room was varying shades of blue. Cerulean for the ceiling, navy for the walls, cyan for the carpet. They were on the inside of some sea-colored jewel. Someone had placed glow-in-the-dark stars on the ceiling, making random constellations. The stars glowed faintly, pale green. They nuzzled, kissed and bit for a while, the boy half-naked, him fully clothed. When enough sweat had generated, Boy Wonder whispered, "Dude…", indicating that Oliver should remove his clothing. They parted, not completely breaking contact. He gripped a pale forearm as he removed his clothing, one-handed and using kicks and toes to assist him. When he got to his underwear, he had to let go. "Here, let me," and the blond head peeled back soaked cotton and buried itself in tangy-scented public hair. Oliver closed his eyes, feeling. The sucking sounds, the smells, the softness of the futon all reminded him of the sea. He fell back, listening and stroking hair, unbelieving. An occasional warm drop of saliva would foam on his thighs.

"Hey, let me…" he murmured. They switched positions. In his mouth, Boy Wonder had no taste. As he pleasured him, Oliver found himself developing a rhythm. Oceanic, tidal. A fan played light breezes on his back. His dark hands cradled buttocks, moans were animal and aerial: the cries of gulls. *What music should be playing?* Oliver thought the question a voice outside his head, one mocking, teasing. But the answer came to him in his own inner voice, so it couldn't have been external. The answer formed into the sound of that music. Echoed, flanged guitar, swooping over watery bass and briny synth. No words to disturb the churning, oozing liquid feel: Cocteau Twins, or Slowdive. The music would have to be mythic and sexy at once. *Good answer*, came the reply. Oliver ignored it, drowning in surf and sand. Opening his eyes, Boy Wonder was foam, the sea at night. He molded him out of sand. Then Boy Wonder rode him like a surf-board. Oliver was hurtled beneath the waves, into himself. The stars on the ceiling floated far up, a layer of increasingly murky water separating him from them. The voices and the music were muffled, like a speaker system that has the bass turned up too high. He dove into the flesh, the spirit. Boy Wonder straddled him as he dove deeper, music and salt and beat.

Oliver nibbled a finger, tasting it. Bone and blood and white. It was a taste that he couldn't get enough of, it was irresistible. *What do you look like on the inside?* T-count, corpuscle, cell: they flashed on the screen of his mind, like names of bands on an MTV commercial. If Boy Wonder bled, would the blood be red, or white, the milky blood of dead fireflies? Would he have bones of calcium, or coral? Red coral, dark pink coral, the color of petals. And his eyes would taste of cool metal, sweet and icy at once. Inside him, Oliver felt the pulse and the beat. Oliver was flesh, dark, impure, and he was now with an elemental. Fucking the sea. He laughed and came with a shudder. And when he came, he thought of alabaster flesh, silver pubic hair, and fragrant coconuts.

"Dude, that was good. Now I'm gonna—"

Oliver looked to see anguished facial expression. When the first ejaculation hit him, he saw eyes open, wide and blue in terror. Then the ejaculations wouldn't stop. It seemed his chest was decorated with splatters of something thick, syrupy and red, like grenadine. Boy Wonder screamed, as blood and cum, milky white and dark red ropes of the two liquids, flew out of his penis. Oliver gasped and screamed as well. The music playing in his head went into high gear, a 33 record played at 45rpm. Guitars were shrill, the beat frantic. It went on and on, forever, gore seeping out of the glans. Then Boy Wonder stopped screaming. He whimpered a little, before the light in his eyes went out. He fell over, dead weight. He smelled sweet and rotten.

Shivering, Oliver lay beneath the body for a good while. He couldn't tell if the body above him was breathing or not. He pushed the boy off of him, and went for his clothes. He sopped up the syrupy mess on his chest with his shirt. He didn't want to know what it was. He got his clothes on in a hurry, and crashed the door open. He was sick to his stomach, and on leaving the room of ocean, was sick. Fire, beer, and Ramen noodles rushed out. The music stopped.

Wiping his mouth on his arm, Oliver ran down the stairs. He saw a group of kids, passed out in front of a TV, blindly groping each other. The TV was on, snow buzzed on the screen, black, blue and silver. The door wasn't locked, so he had no trouble bolting out into the night, shoving past the sidewalk and through the wisps of tattered lace-smoke.

Oliver had made the call at a payphone, outside his dormitory building, in the gray and yellow dawn. "There's a dead kid, somewhere in a house north of Little Italy. I don't have the address." And the horrified hang-up, as he considered the call might be traced. Pompeii had dragged him out of bed by knocking on his door insistently, and holding him when had babbled incoherently about a boy coming blood. It was evening now, the blue and the gold wedding each other in the sky. It was a bad trip, that was all.

"Listen, honey," Pompeii said between dramatic, Garboesque puffs of smoke. "I didn't hear about no death or nothing in the evening news; he was just tripping. You sure you wasn't on something?"

"Yeah," Oliver said miserably.

"Well, you had been drinking."

"Just a couple of beers."

"I don't know. I give up. I just think you were freaking out over something and what seemed like one thing was really another."

They sat in a small café on Charles Street, sipping iced lattes and eating pastries. Pompeii had taken a couple of bird-like nibbles of his chocolate-hazelnut torte and was done with it ("A girl has to watch her figure"). Oliver had dismantled the levels of his napoleon; his fork made gentle fractures in the zebra-striped top. He ate listlessly, chewing, yet not tasting the bitter chocolate and the rich cream.

"I really ought to check it out, just to see if he's okay."

Pompeii shook his head. "No. If something did happen, there'd be all these questions."

"But—"

"Honey. Look, you did what you could: the police were notified, its in their hands. You didn't do anything bad. But the police tend to look for the easiest explanations, and if you go walking right in there. I mean, that's if something happened. I'm sure we'll see that boy out again at Hippos, coked out of his mind."

Oliver didn't reply; he knew what he'd seen. The pale blue eyes, open, unseeing. The stains of blood and semen stained his shirt. He'd have to throw it away. It was a shame; it had been one of his favorite shirts.

He started laughing. *I'm such a fucker; a boy's dead and I'm worried about my shirt!*

"Come on, baby, you're laughing like the Joker." Pompeii placed his turmeric hands on his dark ones. They steadied under his touch (he hadn't known they were shaking).

After a few minutes of solemn silence, Pompeii said, "Well, you can tell me one thing. Was he good?"

"Oh, yes." Boy Wonder had been… wonderful. He remembered the pale blue eyes when they'd been alive. A petrified ocean that he'd dived into. Oliver didn't tell Pompeii about the music, or the voices. (Maybe he had been on something, but just forgotten it. Everyone in that dank, smelly house had been on drugs. When he'd been deep into the scene, he would lose whole days.)

"Well, let me tell you about Cameron…" Pompeii leaned forward, his eyes eager.

Oliver dutifully sat through a tale of debauchery.

"It's hardly a *Twin Peaks* kinda of night, like you had, but I had a good time," Pompeii finished up.

Oliver cracked a grin. "That reminds me of something else weird, that happened that night."

"I hope it doesn't end in death."

"Not at all. I met this other guy, a real strange one. He was an albino. You couldn't have missed him. He had silver hair and was wearing a Coil T-shirt."

Pompeii shook his head.

"Well, he came up to me, and talked to me—"

"Was he cute?"

"He was—"

"Baby, don't say he was 'beautiful'; that's so Anne Rice."

"Well, he was. But, it was strange."

Pompeii looked expectantly at him.

"I always had a thing for albinos," Oliver said. "When I was young, about five or so, a white family moved into a house in our neighborhood. They were very '70s crunchy-liberal: the dad had a ponytail, the mother always wore Indian-patterned skirts. They had a son, who was albino. I remember the first time I saw him, I was scared. I thought that he was a vampire, or something. He was always in dark clothes, even on the hottest days, and he didn't seem to have any veins. He wore dark sunglasses, pitch-black, the kind you see folks in Civil Rights pictures wearing. My brother told me that; but I soon figured out that he couldn't be a vampire, 'cause he was walking out in the sunlight. 'Oh, he's a vampire, all right,' Ken said; he was a real dick, 'he's a new breed. He takes a special serum that allows him to stay in the sunlight. I read about it somewhere.' I didn't believe him. He dared me to take off his sunglasses. 'His eyes will be all shriveled and pink, like a bunny-rabbits' eyes.' I told Ken that I didn't believe him. 'Oh, you're just scared.' The upshot of the story is that one day, I went up to him—all white like an alien—and I knocked his glasses off. Ken had been wrong: Silver's eyes were just blue. But instead of running away, I just stared at him. I was mesmerized. He got up slowly, found his glasses, and put them back on. He walked away without saying a word…"

Oliver took a swig of latte. "After that, we never really saw him around. Oh, now and then. All the kids thought he was some kind of ghoul or something. Thanks to Ken, and his friend Steve, they spread stories. Steve was from a Muslim family; he'd always be talking about white devils, and evil Dr. Yacub. He told the kids in the neighborhood that the creatures the doctor made were white, like that kid. And for some reason--"

"You fell in love with the devil." Pompeii finished for him.

Oliver laughed. "Not quite Anne Rice. His eyes… they're a shade of blue, kind of like… What's that flower? They're that color."

Pompeii pondered for a moment. "I don't know; I may be a fag, but I'm not a florist!"

He laughed again. Pompeii could chase away the shadows. They finished up their pastries and coffee. Every now and then, Pompeii would sing a verse or two of a Madonna song under his breath. It was an annoying habit, but it made Oliver felt safe.

Oliver turned over the Weird Book of the Week: *Yargo*, Jaqueline Susann's last novel. It was a science fiction romance story, between an Earth woman and her extraterrestrial lover. Oliver carried it, with his other finds: *Shadow of the Torturer* and *The Art of Dali*. Nuclear Books was small and cramped, its carpet red and dusty. The shelves were disordered and haphazardly arranged. Vague jazz drifted throughout the store, a musical scent that was mournful and musty at once. It was the perfect refuge for a gray, rainy day. The store was empty—odd for a Saturday. He sauntered over to the comic shelf, where he looked at old R. Crumb and new Gaiman books with longing. But no, these books and the CDs that he'd bought earlier would have to do for now. He still had to get art supplies later.

When he saw him—Silver—walk into the store, he couldn't say that he was exactly surprised; such an environment was natural for him. Oliver felt more relieved.

Silver didn't look all that surprised to see him, either. He was in a shirt that looked like chain mail, loosely knitted. His black jeans were creased; you could cut bread on them. His shoes were shiny. He smiled at Oliver as he removed his headphones.

"Hey. Told you we'd meet."

"Yeah."

"What are you gonna buy?" He grabbed Oliver's wrist, and took the books away. When the contact ceased, there remained a bracelet of cold. "Give me de Chirico any day," he said to the Dali book. "Valley of the Dolls, right? And what's this 'Torturer' thing, eh? He looks awfully fearsome, in a heavy metal kind of way."

"The author of that book, he wrote an introduction to a comic book."

Silver nodded, as if in approval. "I'm gonna have a look around."

"Okay. Nice seeing you again—"

"You leaving?"

It was an invitation. "Not right away."

They split up, he went back to the science fiction section, Silver-Breath to Philosophy or Architecture. Oliver scanned and ignored cheap paperback trilogies. The pale man pored over books with abstract covers and titles. He had put his headphones back on; if Oliver listened closely, he could make out meaningless bits of music, in miniature.

"Hey, Oliver," Silver called out, a little to loud. He laughed with embarrassment as he peeled the plugs from his ears. "Come over here," was softly spoken.

As Oliver walked across the expanse from Fiction to Philosophy, he made a conscious effort not to seem like an over-eager puppy.

Silver held an elegant, slender volume in hand. "This something you oughta read." He offered it to him. "Baudrillard" (the r's were dramatically rolled) "writes about the subjectivity of desire like no-one else."

Oliver accepted the book, and put it with his others.

Silver moved away to another section of the store: Erotica. He'd plugged up his ears again. Oliver followed him. He tapped him on the shoulder.

"What!" then, "what?" a couple of decibels lower.

"I- I was just wondering what you were listening to."

A phone was pressed into his ear. Industrial drumming, quasi-symphonic synth, and a little girl, reciting words in what sounded like French. "Sacrilege! Sacrilege!" she shrieked in her bird-voice, then the sound was ripped out of him. "It was the Cranes."

"Oh, I've heard of it, but I could never—"

"I know, you just love the Cranes. I like the music, but I can't stand her voice; she sounds like Betty Boop trying to be Diamanda Galas. With a few exceptions, I find the whole ethereal girl-singer thing to be tired. I mean, punk was trying to get away from picture-perfect aesthetics. Now we've come full circle. And the take on women, as naïve fairy-children, or mystical goddesses... Why are you laughing?"

"I think it's really weird that you have the wherewithal to insult my taste, but you can't even tell me your name." Oliver walked away. He put the books on the reshelving cart. The game they were playing was just too much.

He was out on the street, heading towards the Art Institute's bookstore, when Silver stopped him.

"I'm sorry," he said. "It was just... I didn't want to piss you off so much. Here." The albino handed him a crumpled bag full of books. "They're on me."

Oliver accepted the bag. It was red, like grenadine.

"My name is John Cane, really boring. My friends call me Silver, for obvious reasons. I grew up in California, mostly the Bay Area, with a stint in Utah. There's not that much to tell. I saw your work once, at the Institute. That stuff you did with those found objects, in the little boxes, I thought it was cool. They were like miniature theaters. That's when I learned about who you were. That's all. Not so mysterious."

Oliver thought back to that show. His little boxes full of wires, covered and exposed, with black icons—doll-sized gods and goddesses—trapped among them. He tried to remember if he'd seen Silver there. In between the glib comments ("It represents the commodification of Black Culture," one critic declared), and college-gallery food (spears of raw vegetables, a melting wheel of Brie, and jugs of wine) he had no memory of him.

"Now come on, man, I don't want you mad at me." Silver removed his glasses. The eyes were revealed, naked and the color of nightshades. Oliver fell into them.

Before long, he was following Silver into another bookstore. This one was New Age: he could smell it from the incense and sandalwood. Everything was clean and bright. Some watered-down appropriation of Native American music played on the speakers (*The Wisdom of Coyote* was the title of the CD; both of them laughed at it).

Silver parked himself in front of the aromatherapy counter, inhaling vial after vial. The bottles were minute and stylized, a color like smoky pomegranates. The liquids seemed to steam and swirl in their prisons. It was fake. You were supposed to imagine that you were some High Lord, uncorking a bottle of magic. A simulacrum, to use academic terminology. Like Silver himself.

"Smell this," he demanded. Oliver obeyed. Eucalyptus stung his nose. They went through scent after scent, until Oliver felt intoxicated. Some were sharp, others so subtle that he could barely detect them. "It's sexy, isn't? Better than poppers," said Silver.

It didn't seem so odd, that his real name (or almost-real name) was the same as the one Oliver had made for him. The whole thing was unreal, anyway. With the fragrances exploding in his brain, Oliver no longer cared anymore. This strange angel was as much a creation of his mind as the boy who came blood. They were from the same place. Who cared? This real-life trip was better than that other one. The gush of blood onto beautiful skin, the rush of smell into his head. Glans, glands.

"You remind me of someone," said Oliver, drunk on bottled vapors.

Silver smiled. "Look, I've got to be going. I have an appointment with an acupuncturist." He held up a bottle of some shimmery oil. When he paid for it, he left the store without looking back.

The throngs of club-kids twisted and swirled their anorexic bodies to deep house, drums 'n bass, and acid jazz. In silver, green and blue, in spandex and lycra, with straight and crimped hair, they were post-modern fairies. They embraced every era and rejected them simultaneously: bell-bottoms and Birkenstocks competed with combat boots and ripped T-shirts, void of contradiction, or even competition, really. They were beautiful, young and vapid. "Beatific" would be their spiritual classification, according to a role-playing game that Oliver had played, long ago. Centaurs in polyester, elementals in platforms. Like the dryads and nymphs of that imaginary realm, they were oblivious to him. He was here because goth bored him, with its stupid pretension; and gay-only places were fascist, filled with assholes. "Nazi FuckBoys" was what he called them. These New-Age discos, however, had very little baggage. They were clean and relatively good-natured, maybe because of the E people were taking.

Oliver sipped his 'smart drink': wheat-grass infused with bee-pollen. It tasted green and insect-like, appropriately. There was something in it, obviously, to tone down the wild flavors. But in spite of the raw taste, he was getting some kind of buzz from it. Whatever it was, Oliver felt the urge to dance. There was no music, only beat. Occasionally something recognizable would come on, a bit of Annie Lennox or Björk, but the melodies and voices would be remixed, sacrificed to the god of dance.

The crowd moved as one, in love with itself. Each spaced-out whoosh and whir of the music brought a member deeper into the collective trance. The women were dolls, with porcelain faces and jewelry eyes; you could buy them on the Shopping Network, and display them on mirror-stands. They were dolls; not the strong dark goddesses that he'd imprisoned in his boxes of snake-wires. Put these little white girls in the nest of vipers, and they'd be devoured. The boys, however, were something more. They were perfect specimens, like the figures in medical books. Flip one page, and you'd see (through transparent flesh) the muscle structure. Flip another page, and organs, fabulous coloring-book shapes, were revealed. You could flip, through tissue and tendon, until only bone was left. It was putrescence without the baggage of rot. Was that what had come out of Boy Wonder's dick? Throwing himself into the sea of them, Oliver wanted to rip layer after layer off the beatific boys. There was a moment when he felt that he was being unfair, but then he remembered. In the gaming manual it had stated that those with a "Beatific" alignment were essentially naïve, and amoral. They could kill at any moment, and not feel the slightest regret. Centaurs have teeth, and diamond-sharp hooves.

The music he was dancing to was soulless, meaningless. It didn't even pretend to have emotion. It was something that Silver might've commented on, in his odd, theoretical way.

"He's a mindfucker," was Pompeii's assessment of him, after hearing Oliver's story. "He doesn't give a shit about you. I'll even bet it's that same albino kid, after all these years, trying to get you back at you."

Oliver agreed with him—partially.

"I know that he's all fucked up; I still find him fascinating." To Pompeii's unasked why: "I don't know. It's just—I can't explain it. Sorry."

"You just watch yourself."

In the flashing, glitter-light of a disco ball, Oliver wondered what about paleness was so seductive? All the other boys were nothing next to Silver.

In the shifting, punctuated light, borne on faceless music, a faceless boy drifted over. Faceless because the boy looked like all the others: pretty, thin, standard-issue gym body. Though Oliver wasn't a very good dancer, whites imposed the spirit of rhythm on him. So he became the Jungle personified and danced with the faceless boy.

Oliver forced himself to memorize this boy's face, his hair. He could've been Boy Wonder, or any of the boys in front of him. Sandy-brown hair, blue eyes.

The two of them danced until Oliver's legs hurt, until sweat ran down his brow.

"Hey," said the faceless boy, "you're pretty good." He, of course, wasn't sweating. Instead, he was laved in a golden sheen. "James," he said, pointing to himself.

"Oliver."

"You don't come 'round here much. You new, bro?" James asked.

He knew where the conversation would end up. The delicate meandering around the eventual goal was exhilarating, if perplexing. First Boy Wonder, then this guy. Why did they suddenly want him?

They talked about music (James was into techno), and Oliver's studies at the Maryland College of Art.

"Man, I think that shit is cool. You're a fuckin' artist. I mean, I'm inta computers an' shit, you know, cybershit. But it ain't nothin' like drawin' shit."

They danced some more.

Finally, at closing time: "Do you want to come home with me, bro? I don't live too far from here."

The two walked a couple of blocks to a basement apartment in silence. James was flush with excitement; Oliver could see his nipples were hard. Oliver himself was full of dread; but his lust overcame it. It had been three weeks since the death, the details receding in his mind. The memory had a trippy quality. Maybe Pompeii was right, he'd taken something earlier, had forgotten about it.

"This is a mess," said James, after they were inside. It was. Mounds of balled up clothes were on the floor, spots of the drab carpet showing through. A pallet lay in the center of the room. The walls were forest green, hung with posters of computerized landscapes—jungles, beaches, mountains—with futuristic lettering and hieroglyphics on them. Cybernetic organisms, featureless, sleek and created of not-yet-created alloys, were frozen in various poses. One of the poster-cyborgs disturbed him. It was a white face that looked poured: formed of some white liquid that had both the qualities of ice and clay. The eyeless eyes saw. Its subtle mouth grinned. The head floated in a void.

There was no preface, no opening remarks as they removed their clothes in the small room. James knelt in front of him, and took his dick in his mouth. Oliver was enveloped in velvet moistness. He closed his eyes. James stopped, and turned off the lights. When he'd returned, Oliver was on his knees, waiting. "No," said James, "you don't have to do a thing. Not yet." Oliver stood up, was again in his mouth. An upstairs neighbor put some music on. It was techno of the bass and drums variety. It thudded downwards into the room, his brain. Muffled, aroused, Oliver analyzed it, deconstructing the beat. Dark bass tones covered, then frittered away, to reveal the naked bone of rhythm, which, after all, did not have structure. The music was appropriate, pornographic. He groaned. Behind his lids, things formed. Liquid white and speckled dark, the leaves of a jungle of electronics and sound. Pale antelopes, made of 0s and 1s, bounded before him. Whirring insects, machines morphed of special effects, buzzlessly flew. He gripped James's shoulders and shoved his head forward. He made him gag on his dick, before releasing him.

Gasping, James said, "Fuck me." A while later, he entered James, through membranes and lubrication. The music above seemed to get louder. They perspired. Grunting, he was in the jungle again. The fetid scents filled his nostrils, screeches filled his ears: real or sampled? He opened his eyes, looking at the form he impaled. The head in the poster stared. It encouraged him. The piece of music above him was now slower, dubbed out, filled with echo and spaces of silence between the beats. It got hotter in the room. There was an organic smell in the small room, of overripe mangos, bananas, and vegetation. And flesh. It was sweet, the smell of the golden boy's flesh, like all those fruits, and more. Blood, like nectar, the flesh tender like a peach. Even the bad parts, the shit and the urine, would be inoffensive, when devoured.

He knew what was happening, but he couldn't stop it. He didn't want to. When James climaxed, he exploded. This time, it was different. Blood burst underneath the tan skin, and oozed away in a beautiful, watercolor saturation of pink and red. He was a living, giant peach, for a moment. His eyes were open, the blue eyes floating in liquid, pickled.

Oliver calmly extracted his dick from the dead boy. The condom was covered in shit. He peeled it off, and stroked himself. He came, thick and pale, onto the corpse.

He had known, even before he went into the club, what was going to happen.

He washed up listlessly. Already, the scent of perfume filled the room. James the peach was melting, sweetly. Before he stepped from the room, he saw the odd poster staring at him. The head had deformed, melted. It was now a fabulous, formless white blob.

When he left the apartment, the room of synthesized jungle, he heard no music. Maybe there had been no music at all.

Baltimore at 3 a.m. was silent and clammy. The streets had cracks and fissures like burst capillaries. He walked them, without feeling or thought. The blocks went by. A hint of green appeared at the edge of the sky, changing the sky from black to darkest indigo. On a corner, there was a diner, its lights cheerfully on. He walked inside.

Everything was bright. The countertops, booths and stools were candy-apple red, accented by white and gray borders. The silver buttons gleamed. Disembodied music—syrupy strings, gentle, crooning tenor, and oceanic, "ahh"-ing female choir—blasted out of a jukebox. He headed for a counter, catching a flash of white in the corner of his eye. When he turned, he saw that the white thing he saw was man-shaped.

It didn't really surprise him to see Silver in this diner. He seemed to bookend disaster.

Silver waved him over to his booth. "Oliver, I was just thinking of you. Fancy, meeting you here. Must be telepathy."

Oliver slumped across from him.

Silver went on: "This place is great. 4 a.m., you get all types here. Great place for inspiration. And—" he leaned close, "the waitresses here all look like fat drag queens. You'll see."

One such elephantine woman took his order (a roughly grunted "coffee" he didn't recall saying); her peach-pink uniform was tight against her girth, her hair piled into an impossible beehive, with a cloth flower stuck into its apex.

Silver babbled on: "I bought you something. I've been carrying it around since I got it, in case we ran into each other." The song changed to some smoky female singer against a swaying samba. "I think you'll appreciate it." He slid a book across the table. *The Story of the Eye*. A pickled blue eyeball glared at Oliver from a swirl of flesh-colored smoke.

Oliver retched, each spasm painful and sharply felt. What was inside him came out. Except there was nothing left inside of him. Silver laid hands on his back. The ice chilled him, soothed him. The retching subsided. He was only hyperventilating now. When that ceased, he had his coffee in front of him.

"Easy. I had no idea that you felt so strongly about Bataille."

"I," he gasped, "I just saw someone die…."

Silver didn't react. In fact, he didn't seem all that surprised. Johnny Mathis mewled over a thousand sea-sick violins. The jukebox colors glowed, lozenges of pastel pink, mint, and lemon. The drag-queen waitresses patrolled their domain in luxuriant slow motion.

"It wasn't what you wanted?"

Oliver stared at him. "What do you mean?"

"You know what I mean. All those boys. Those 'Nazi Fuck-boys.'" (How did he know?) "You got what you wanted from them, then they got what they deserved. What you wanted."

"What are you talking about?"

This was not real, this conversation. Once he acknowledged this, it was possible to continue, to say anything.

Silver looked annoyed. "I gave you what you wanted," he said in slow tones, as if speaking to a child.

They were interrupted by the behemoth-waitress. She placed a slab of lemon meringue pie in front of Silver. The meringue was like a strange mushroom: the top part blackened, the underneath pale colorless foam. The filling quivered like jellied urine.

Following the metaphysical thread of the conversation, Oliver said, "I wanted you. Why didn't you sleep with me? Those others were just stand-ins."

Silver mashed the disturbing pie into his mouth, turning his teeth bright yellow. "You can't have sex with Want."

Oliver laughed. "You're losing me here. You're saying that you are Desire with a capital D? That's fucked up."

Silver made a great, fussy show of wiping his lips with a napkin. His breath—cold yet sugary—drifted over to Oliver. "Consider the word vanilla. When you think of vanilla, you think of white ice-cream, bland, boring. White bread. But the source of vanilla is a bean that's black."

Laughing, Oliver shook his head. Silver continued: "In order for anything to become really pale, it has to be in a place where no light comes. It must be in the dark."

"Ridiculous. Fucked up. Pompeii told me you were a user, a fuck." Oliver stood up, reached into his wallet, and threw down a dollar. It missed the table. "Don't talk to me again, you fucking freak. My brother was right; you are a devil."

The denouement of "These Boots Are Made For Walking" blared out of the speakers, a fanfare of horns and kitsch. The waitress moved by in trance, oblivious as a blimp. He stomped out of the diner. When the door banged shut, he heard no sound. Nothing. When he turned back, the lights of the diner were off.

It was abandoned.

Miles Davis issued in shades of blue from his speakers. The sound bounced off his dorm room walls. The curtains were drawn against the soupy gray light of outside. In the semi-dark, Oliver worked intently on his project. The gods and goddesses—orishas and loas—were freed from their prison of wires and industrialization, and elevated on pedestals of black marble, wood, and brass. They wore royal robes, and were surrounded by their familiars—toy plastic lions, hyenas, and snakes. He had altered the dolls' faces; they now wore fierce, primeval expressions.

He was in the middle of making a robe for the Afro-Brazillian sea goddess Iemanja, cutting a sheet of sapphire cloth, when someone knocked on the door.

"Just a minute." He put down the scissors, and walked over to the door. "Who is it," he said.

"Just open the door, girl. I've been knocking for-fucking-ever!"

Standing in the door frame, Pompeii wore a black muscle T-shirt and tight, forming-fitting gray jeans. His head was freshly shorn, and a ruby stud sparkled in his nose. It had been a while since Oliver had seen him.

"Where have you been, girl?"

"Busy," Oliver answered. "I'm working on a new project. I haven't had time to hang out."

Pompeii let himself in. Oliver hesitated before closing the door after his entrance.

"It's been a month. Look at you, girl! You've gone all ethnic, and shit. What's this you have on—a dashiki? Kente cloth? And you're playing—what is this? Where's Joy Division and Christian Death?" Pompeii had flopped himself on the bed. "I hope you haven't become one of those born-again black people."

At first, Oliver ignored him. Then he began to get pissed off. What right did he have to judge him? Besides, if Pompeii only knew—

Just as he was about to yell at him, Pompeii said, "Look. I've been worried about you." His tone was serious. "I mean, ever since you told me about, you know, I've just been…."

Oliver stared at him.

"I mean, you had a some kind of, I don't know, breakdown or something. I respect space, and everything. But. Don't leave your friends outside, Okay?"

"I did not have a breakdown."

"Oliver, boys don't die by melting or cumming blood. You can't kill anyone by having sex with them. You don't have that power."

"Fuck you. You didn't see…." He was choking on something. Tears. The words gasped out. He didn't know what he was saying. All he knew was that suddenly, he was in Pompeii's arms, wheezing against his expensive shirt. Probably ruining it. But Pompeii pressed him closer, until the wave of emotion subsided.

"This Silver guy, he really fucked with your mind."

"But—"

"Oliver! Listen. I didn't hear one damn thing about mysterious deaths. Not one thing. What does that tell you? And this get up. You can't get rid of whatever you're going through by pretending to be something that you're not. I think you need to see someone. I'm telling you. I'm gonna nag you until you do. And you know what a bitch I can be!"

Oliver laughed through snot and tears.

Pompeii placed his hand on his shoulders, and began to gently knead them. "Another thing. Take this shit off."

Oliver removed his shirt. Pompeii's hands came in contact with his flesh. He was rippled by a tide of gooseflesh.

"It's gonna be all right," Pompeii murmured. The sound was moist, and intimate.

There was a moment of silence, of inaction, where they both acknowledged what was about to happen, the absurdity of it all. Pompeii pushed Oliver down on his bed, lingered above momentarily before leaning in to kiss him. After the kiss, Pompeii tongued down his neck to his chest, where he began to playfully lap and tug at Oliver's nipples. He was sweet and mysterious. His breath was scented with something spicy. Nutmeg? It was delicious. Pompeii's blood would taste of mulled cider, his flesh, like mincemeat pie filling. The sax shaded everything with the blue-gold of the clouds in Romantic period paintings. Oliver closed his eyes.

White things fluttered behind his lids. Moth wings, with specks of dark-pink. Creatures that could only hide in the darkest closet.

Pompeii grew rougher, gripping and kneading Oliver's cock through his trousers.

Not Pompeii, Oliver thought. He pushed him off. Pompeii fell to the floor as he sat up. He looked sort of dazed. Then, when his eyes got their focus back, there was something burning in them. Something bright.

Pompeii pinned Oliver down on the bed. He bit his neck. His lithe body ground itself against his. Oliver was hard, in spite of himself. Pompeii was so beautiful, now the burnished color of ghee, his flesh hinted at succulence and muted iridescence.

"Not Pompeii! Please."

Pompeii's approach altered. The frantic behavior fell away. His kisses became gentle, even bashful. Oliver's fingers rested on the smooth, amber upturned bowl of Pompeii's head. He closed his eyes again. Moth wings fluttered. He found himself unable to open his eyes, as if there were a weight upon them. But with the sensations on his body, he found that he didn't care that much. He knew that the moths were a manifestation of Silver, of his desire. He pleaded in between bouts of pure pleasure with him. Don't take Pompeii, please. The music changed. The sax fell away, transformed into a woman's voice, soaring over somnambulant architecture. Houses of terra-cotta, open deserts of swirling sand, frost-tinged cacti. Silver promised him this, in exchange for the sacrifice.

Oliver declined.

After Pompeii left, Oliver took a shower, washing semen and sweat off his body. He put on a Swans T-shirt, and black jeans. It was evening, now. The rain-washed scent of Baltimore drifted up to his dorm room.

Silver—or Desire—had listened to him, and spared Pompeii. He considered this.

"You can't have sex with Want," he'd said, that night in the diner.

But he could have sex with what he wanted. All of his life, his desire had been his enemy. The distant, beautiful boys. The "Nazi-Fuckboys." Now, he could have them through some metaphysical loophole.

What he'd reacted to was their deaths, the needless sacrifices, of blood and sperm. But when Oliver thought about it, it made some sense. He had always wanted—desired—to hurt those boys. To make them want him, then leave them, stripped of their beauty. Their deaths were unpleasant, yes. But they were what he wanted.

Oliver stood up, and walked past the orishas. He took *Kind of Blue* out of the CD player, replacing it with *Love's Secret Domain*. It burbled out of the speakers.

Tonight, he'd meet up with Silver, and they would hash out their arrangement. Where would he be? Someplace cool, that much was sure.

If Desire isn't exactly my friend, at least he isn't my enemy.

Her Spirit Hovering

Howard Stone liked the color black. It had many symbolic meanings. Some saw it as an inky darkness, pulsating with swallowed light and energy. Others used it as a representation of Nothing: a great gaping void that a body would be lowered into, devoured by the earth until nothing—no thought, no memory—would remain. The dark had a certain majesty. No wonder it was used to represent the glamour of evil. But there was none of that glamour here. None whatsoever. Sunlight poured through the stained glass windows, drenching the church in crimson, gold and pale green. These joyful, spring-like tones glowed on the pews, the walls, the audience and on the coffin where his mother lay.

A sharp, remorseful sigh escaped from Stone. His eyes blurred momentarily. There lay his mother in a pine box. Her dyed red hair had faded. She was in a black gown with a lily pinned to her dress. A large, gaudy lily made of wax with cloth leaves. Even in death she could be tacky. He felt a pang of guilt; funerals were supposed to be sad occasions. Maybe he would paint a picture for his mother, a visual dirge of mourning elements: thunder, nightshades, warped trees. In the midst of this landscape would be his mother, a graceful, serene Madonna... Stone choked back a laugh. Unlike Whistler's portrait with its elegant, dour subject, Stone's mother would be in a LAZ-Boy, wearing a tube-top and plaid polyester leisure pants.

The pastor nodded at Stone—he was ready to begin. Stone nodded back, and looked at his own hands. They were knotted together in a complex linking of the fingers. He tried to separate them. But they wouldn't part. He tried harder, fearful that he'd have to go through life forever with his hands stuck together, when a soft, gentle hand rested over his and the fingers came unglued, as if by magic. Stone faced the owner of the healing hand—it was one his mother's mahjong partners. He jerked his hands away. He didn't need her help.

A hush went through the church as the eulogy began.

"We are gathered here today to mourn the loss of our dear sister Martha Ann Stone. This should not be a day of sorrow, but one of joy, for our sister has left this harsh world to join the Father. We are all but little children in the hands of God, and our sister Martha has climbed into that great hand..."

Someone moaned and blew their nose quite loudly. A few coughs sounded.

"...was a kind woman, with many good friends and deeds behind her..."

The person moaned again, almost orgasmically, right in his ear. The mahjong partner. Her eyes were red and puffy, and the sounds she made between moans were rough, ugly barks for air. She blew her nose again, emitting a bleating whimper. *Why can't I cry? There was once a time when I did nothing but cry.* Stone searched his body for anguish, but found none. He remembered when he'd cried without abandon, warm salt tears wearing grooves in his skin. He'd been seven years old and playing in the Forbidden Room. This room had an antique bed with a lacy canopy. There was an invisible guardian angel in front of the room, warning him. He ignored the angel. The thick, gothic gloom beckoned. He was so small and pale in his knee-length shorts and striped shirt. The bed was an island of

Chantilly lace floating on a cloud of mahogany. It was irresistible. She was downstairs, working in the basement. He heard his mother even as he crossed the threshold: "Grandma Jenny had this bed from slavery times, when the Stones owned and bred the best Negroes in Jackson, Mississippi. It's a genuine antique."

She'd caught him on the bed, where he was sipping his Ovaltine and lining up his favorite stuffed animals: Tig the tiger with a missing felt eye and Sperba, the gooseberry-green duck, for some fantasy game. His mother spanked him ruthlessly—how dare he disrespect her, her grandmother and her good family's heirlooms! Now Stone thought of the Faulkner story, "A Rose for Emily" whenever he recalled that bed. Instead of a corpse decaying on the bed, he saw three generations of Stone women, every one of them with bad hairdos and dye jobs. Ever since then he'd hated every stick of furniture in that house. The brown and orange leaf-patterned couch. The two black and aqua chairs. There were pictures on the walls—a Virgin Mary and baby Jesus done on velvet, a picture of a father he'd never met. And overseeing her domain was her icon: cat-eye glasses, red hair like a clown's fright wig, lips curled in a smile of quiet acceptance that didn't question.

The pastor's voice broke into his thoughts. "Martha is survived by her sister Thelma Waters, who could not be here today, and a son Howard, an artist whom she supported throughout her life."

Supported! She never supported me! No, I'd earned that scholarship to the Corcoran School of Art. And when I opened his show in Atlanta, and the critics tore it apart, was she supportive? Did she say, "It's wonderful! Those critics wouldn't know artistic genius if it bit them!"? No. The night after those reviews had come in, she said, "Why couldn't you have painted trees? Or a house? Why didn't I paint a tree, Mom? Because I'm not aiming for a Starving Artist sale. I don't want to paint green seascapes, purple mountains and wide-eyed puppy dogs.

After that failure he had a breakdown.

And she had come home one day, dancing with excitement. It seemed that she'd gotten a job interview for him. "It's as an artist!"

Her lipstick had been Popsicle-orange. Her smile had stretched as far as sanity could go.

He should've been afraid, very afraid. He had visions of being a house painter or an art instructor for senior citizens. But it was much worse. He was to interview for a position as an artist at a greeting card company. He declined politely. But she kept harping on it for a week, about how much an opportunity it was. You had to start somewhere, didn't you? "Oh, come on Howard. You've done nothing but sit around the house since you came back from the Cracker Factory."

The guilt had finally gotten to him. He went to the interview with his mainstream portfolio in hand. Something in the pit of his stomach said "no." He ended up getting the job. It paid well, and was mindless. For fifteen years it had distracted him from higher ambitions. In a way, it was Zen to lose yourself in simple strokes and daubs of paint. The drawback? The finished product was a fuzzy animal or an Easter egg nestled in a grassy hiding place. Flowers and fairies, that sort of thing. And he'd have to letter the inscription with things like Happy Birthday or We Offer Our Condolences For You Loss.

Stone was tapped on the shoulder. People rose to view the body. He stood stiffly. People patted, hugged and kissed him. When all of the people in the church had left, and he was alone, Stone knelt beside his mother. He leaned to kiss her, but stopped at the feeling of intimacy so strong it burned. To do this, to kiss her, would be a sign of weakness, an admission of vulnerability. Stone left his mother's corpse and told the pastor that he was ready to go to the gravesite. Pall-bearers closed the coffin lid. There was a cross etched on the pine. He told the four men that he'd like a few minutes alone after all. They nodded in mute sympathy.

Stone stared at the carved cross until it blurred. A lifetime's work, to be buried and rot in the ground!

His masterpiece and his failure had been an artistic interpretation of James Joyce's *Finnegan's Wake*, done as a mixed media work. He'd spent years of painstaking research, forgone relationships, traveled to Ireland, and sacrificed everything for this epic work. After consulting Joycean scholars at Duke, UNC-Chapel Hill and in DC's Georgetown University and his trip to Dublin, he'd drawn hundreds, if not thousands of pictures, each representing words in the language Joyce had created. The end result was a giant Celtic cross made of polished blond wood, about eight feet tall. Within the interlaces were panels depicting scenes from the novel. Modern Dublin (of the '20s) competed with Irish mythology (kelpies, goddesses, and heroes). Permutations of Christianity, allusions to Eliot's *Wasteland*. To have all that work destroyed by the sniping of critics, their reviews unanimous in denouncement. "An ambitious, ill-fated fiasco". "Stone's work… attempts to Greatness with a hubris not often seen… only succeeds in confusing." And the worst: "Stone shoots for the Whitney but ends up in the Utah Museum of Crafts." In rage he'd destroyed the second piece he'd been working on.

The pastor interrupted his reverie. Stone found his fists clenched, and he was sweating.

"Don't worry, son," said the octogenarian pastor, "when a loved one leaves us, they are always with us in our hearts. Your mother isn't gone. In a way, she will never leave you."

Blah, blah, blah. If you only knew how I really felt. For a moment Stone feared that the pastor, like all of the cloth, could read the depths of his soul with a telepathic sense. He left the church, somewhere between guilt and honest anguish. But anguish over what? That he was guilty?

Stone closed the door behind him. It creaked as always. But now that creak had a different meaning, now that she was gone. Everything did. Even her smell—talcum, and alcoholic, flowery perfume—had faded. He sauntered over to the couch and passed by the mirror. There he was, pushing forty, with graying brown hair, salt-and-pepper mustache and glasses. He slicked back his hair and adjusted his silk tie—he'd have to be ready for the guests that would be arriving, bringing their food and sympathy. He gasped—that shocking, garish photograph of his mother's face was opposite the mirror. She leered at him from a Sears sky-blue background and a thicket of plastic flowers. A parody of a daguerreotype, colorized like an old Shirley Temple movie, and instead of some elegant subject, say Evelyn Nesbitt or Sarah Bernhardt, there was just her. Stone shuddered. She was macabre—evil and ridiculous at once. A Grand Guignol character, a Judy puppet. Stone smiled, remembering.

He had to convince her to go to the Corcoran all those years ago. Subterfuge had been the order of the day. He had to outfox her. Ignorant and obstinate, she had an almost supernaturally-tinged sense of suspicion. So he told her that he wanted to be an interior designer, something she could understand and appreciate, even if she was sorely in need of the services of one herself.

"The capitol is overrun by the colored folks," she'd said one night, cracking open peanuts. She would eat them, then root around her mouth with a cocktail toothpick. He tried not to look disgusted as the green cellophane frill skimmed a cigarette stained tooth.

"They shoot and kill each other and destroy property. You sure you wanna go there? We got plenty of good schools down here, where it's safe."

He had played her game. "Oh, I'll move to the suburbs." He'd no intention of doing so.

"An interior designer, eh?" She'd grinned. "One of your Uncle Beau's things was a designer. You sure you're not funny?"

Stone smiled politely at that one. In spite of her contempt for Uncle Beau's—how would she put it? His lifestyle—she had genuine love for her brother. He remembered one summer as a small boy, the three of them sitting on the porch. Stone was smashing flies and mosquitoes against his legs. A bottle of grape Nehi rested next to him; Uncle Beau and his mother sat in wicker chairs with glasses of Electric Lemonade, getting drunk and giggling. The two of them compared the imagined prowess and carnal abilities of various ethnicities. They sent him away when the conversation grew too raunchy and vulgar.

"No, Mom, I'm not like Uncle Beau."

She gazed at him skeptically. "Well, it sure breaks my heart, to see you go."

"Thank you," Stone said, woodenly hugging her frame. He knew that she would appreciate this; scenes like these were supposed to end in hugs, like in the movies. The summer before leaving for DC had been one of the best. Her more vicious tendencies had been curbed, perhaps by the knowledge that he was leaving. He was floating on Cloud Nine, dreaming of future adventures. They had Moments, many of them. Like the Dale Evans and Roy Rogers Festival on TV, where she wore a cowboy hat and waved a toy gun at the cathode-ray screen. It was silly and endearing. He would never see it again; he was determined not to. So her annoying ticks had become quaint eccentricities.

That's right. Just remember the good times.

But he just couldn't. The lies about where he was living—"Mom, Rockville is just too far from the school; I had to take an apartment on Q Street… Yes, its a safe neighborhood. Yes, there are plenty of white people here. Did I say plenty? I meant the entire block is white."—had haunted his existence. Never mind that he was living in the area where the luminaries of the Harlem Renaissance once held their living room courts. The ghosts of Hurston, Bontemps, Toomer and Hughes didn't linger there; the ghoulish doppleganger of his mother did with the constant threat of appearing unannounced. Which she did one time.

The doorbell rang.

Howard glanced at her grinning, frozen face on the wall. "You have exactly two hours; make the most of it. Afterwards you'll be replaced by a Kahlo or an O'Keefe." He laughed. But he felt eyes burning the nape of his neck as he headed toward the door.

The boxes were unexpectedly heavy even though they were filled with paperbacks and magazines. Stone was sweating by the time he had moved several from the basement to the back of his station wagon. The contents of these boxes were more appropriate souvenirs of Martha Stone's essence than anything else. Lurid romance novels with busty heroines embraced by bronzed, shirtless men. Tabloids that had large-eyed, pale aliens, has-been movie actresses and fad diets. These would go straight to Goodwill. With each trip outside her portrait appraised him. He'd yet to take the picture down. On the fifth trip from the basement he rested, looking at his mother.

"Don't look at me like that," he muttered. "It's my goddamned house now."

There was no response. The way it should've been all along.

On the seventh trip upstairs he stumbled. Books spilled onto the carpet. Stone swore, and began placing them back into the box. One of the covers showed an Anglicized "Indian" princess. *The Passion of a Cheyenne Heart.* Then he recalled with shame the time he'd bought Kamela back from school for Thanksgiving. She was from India. Her skin had the sheen of oil and her lacquered black hair was woven into a thick, heavy braid. A classmate from the Corcoran, she was also his first girlfriend. The sight of her unbound hair flowing around her shoulders, like some sorceress', still made him weak. When his mother had answered the door, he saw the pursed, frosted lips, the scowling eyes behind their cat-eye lenses. Howard, I thought you was going to bring home a nice white girl. Instead, you bought home this. But her initial hostility dampened. After all, Martha Stone was Southern and charm was the South's stock and trade. Mint juleps and refrigerator cookies were passed around. Stone ignored his mother's inane chatter. The rise and fall of Kamela's breasts beneath her turtleneck mesmerized him; he'd held them last night. He thought of her form beneath, then on top of his. Her hair lashing wildly. The elegance of her British delivery, like an NPR announcer's.

Then came the crashing blow, the moment that Stone was sure his mother was waiting for.

"What exactly is your—uh—ethnicity?" Martha Stone had the ubiquitous cellophane toothpick poised in her fingers. Her fingernails, her press-on claws, were painted pink to match her lipstick.

"I'm Indian—"

His mother raised her palm and held it perpendicular to her body. "How!" And she laughed maniacally.

Kamela began to giggle, out of politeness. "Actually, I'm from just outside New Delhi."

Stone had buried his face in his hands.

Later, Martha Stone had explained, "Oh, Howard, she did said she was an Indian."

He apologized to Kamela for his mother's display of ignorance. Kamela insisted she wasn't offended. "She's charming, really." But he knew she'd been insulted. Afterwards, he couldn't face her again and broke it off.

Stone sat on the living room floor, the coarse carpet making him itch, his lower left leg asleep from the angle in which it was resting. He was slightly flushed from remembering Kamela's beauty. *You took that away from me.* He could've had two beautiful brown children with shining agate eyes and hair; and a wife who now worked in the Asian Art Department of the Smithsonian. But, like his art, that was gone. No thanks to his mother.

Stone brought up another one box. *The Wiles of a Vixen* peeked up at him. A Victorian governess in a scarlet mantle ran through a forest of bare silver birch, grinning, pursued by her brooding gypsy lover.

Stone's second lover, Ned, had insisted, "Your mother's a scream." Ned was pale and thin, and had some mysterious aristocratic past. Stone imagined that Ned's father was the patriarch of an industrialist family. Ned had done something to offend them, whether his homosexuality or past experiences with drugs, or perhaps a combination of both. Stone thought this because Ned's mother would whisper into the phone when she called. As if she was afraid she'd be caught. His father never called. Whatever the offense was, it wasn't great enough to stop sending the boy to the Corcoran with a nice living stipend.

Ned could've been an albino, he was so pale. He didn't have blood, he had ichor. Except in really cold weather, when a curious, teacup-shaped spot of bright red appeared on just his right cheek. If he wasn't one of the Beautiful People, he was a distant relation. During Stone's junior year, they shared an apartment on Capitol Hill, near Eastern Market. A townhouse basement with milky-blue walls, a kitchenette, and a queen-sized bed with mounds of fluffy pillows. Ned's unseen mother provided the rent and all the furniture. Both Stone's nascent sculptures and Ned's charcoal sketches—self-described as "a cross between Erte and Dr. Seuss"—adorned the walls and, in some cases, the floors of their nest. Stone blushed, recalling the afternoons spent exploring Ned's marble icon of a body. But even that Martha Stone had taken from him.

The day that began the end of his relationship with Ned started so excellent. Stone awoke to streaks of golden sunlight hitting the bowl of fruit he was going to use as a still-life model. Ned awakened next to him, his white-blond hair tousled, silver-gray eyes reflecting an image of him, and murmuring "Howie." After sex they ate sourdough pancakes with real maple syrup (a gallon had magically appeared, via UPS, the day before. "The fairy's godmother again," Ned had said). Someone knocked on the door.

"Expecting someone, Howie?"

Both of them were bare-chested and in their pajama bottoms. Ned stood and walked toward the door. Stone had a horrible premonition. His Aunt Thelma lived in Norfolk, Virginia, a good two hours from DC; his mother had spoken to him last week about driving up to visit her and her nephew the Klansman. What if, on a lark, she decided—

"Ned, don't!"

"Calm down, Howie. Both of us are comely; let's give 'em a dose of good old queer domescity." And he opened the door.

Like the slowed-down scene of a grade B horror film, the door swung back. The camera panned back, revealing layers of pleated, floral printed polyester, a carnival wig of maraschino cherry-red curls, and like a dollop of whipped cream, a Jackie O pillbox hat. Without a word, Ned turned to Stone with a wide grin splitting his face. Stone hated him from that moment onward.

"You must be Mrs. Stone." Ned bent down gallantly, inviting her in. "I'm Ned Meniscus, Howie's—Howard's roommate. Welcome to our humble—very humble abode."

The witch stepped in with a "How nice you are."

A speechless Stone sat staring. She walked over and hugged him (he'd forgotten to stand until the last moment). After an inspection littered with niceties and small talk, Martha Stone settled down to business: the criticism of her son's life.

"This is what you do?" she asked, looking at an abstract sculpture that he'd labored on.

"Yes. Why don't you have a seat? Can I offer you some water?"

"Oh, yes, dear, of course. Just look at Ed's artwork, though; it's as cute as the Dickens. I know plenty of folks who'd want that sorta stuff, those peculiar lookin' people in colorful outfits." Ned beamed. "But this. This just looks like a rock with some sort of a stick peeking out of it. What in tarnation is it?"

"It's an abstract sculpture, Mrs. Stone, and it's the latest rage. I hear of several stars—Lee Majors and Suzanne Sommers—who collect them. They just can't get enough of them." Did Ned have to be so queeny? And it was one thing if *he* were condescending to his mother.

"Really," came his mother's incredulous reply.

The conversation turned to other things. "You fellas share a single bed. Don't you think that's a little, uh, you know?"

Ned improvised while Stone looked horrified: "Well, Howie's, I mean Howard's bed has seen better days. One day, it just collapsed.

I told him to buy a new bed-frame, not that monstrosity from the church bazaar. But he wouldn't listen to me. It's a temporary arrangement, this bed-sharing."

She'd been eager to suck up that lie. As the two of them chatted about this and that, Stone felt left out and disgusted at the both of them. When his mother bought up the issue of blacks and crime in the city, Ned had obliged her, like indulging a sweet-natured, but dim-witted child. As evening fell, Stone and his mother went to dinner together.

"I want some real food, none of this hoity-toity city food. Something down-home and simple."

He took her to the Florida Avenue Grill, a tight, narrow greasy-spoon that specialized in Southern Soul Food. The two of them sat at the Formica counter and ate crispy fried chicken iridescent with oil, cornbread sweet as cake, greens swimming in pot liquor and macaroni and cheese.

Martha said, "As Beau and me often said, colored folks can do a few things right, and cooking is one of 'em."

"Shhh," hissed Stone.

He glanced around at the clientele, mostly blacks and white college students, to see if they'd overheard. His mother blushed slightly. It was a form of Tourette's Syndrome, really, her habit of blurting out ignorant things. She had no control.

She told him about her trip to Aunt Thelma's and her tour of the Navy yards. As they were getting ready to leave, she said, "Tell me the truth, Howard. That Ned is a funny boy."

"He's nice—" Stone blurted out.

"Oh, I'm sure. But sleeping in the same bed with him—he hasn't tried anything, has he? Here." She pressed a wad of bills into his palm as they left the restaurant. "Get yourself a new bed as soon as you can."

She left him at the door to his home. He waved her off. Then he went into the house, steaming mad. He was greeted by a half-naked Ned, thoughtfully chewing on a kumquat.

"Your mother's a scream! She's like a John Waters character—"

"What do you mean?" Howard's voice had been low.

"I mean, she's endearing, kind of like a drag—"

"Listen to me, Ned. My mother is not some camp belle. She's a monster."

"Oh, come on, Howie. She's not that bad; when you consider where and when she's grown up—"

"Enough! You of all people…" Howard glared at Ned. Traitor. For the next week he wouldn't speak to Ned. How could he like his mother so much? At the end of the week, he came home from the class he T.A.'d, and found his belongings—a trunk full of clothing, a suitcase of art supplies—sitting outside. Ned opened the door. He looked ravishing in a black turtleneck and dark jeans. He was a Beat Angel.

Before Stone could open his mouth, Ned said, "I sent your artwork over to the school; I don't know if they got it or not. I'd like the key back."

He smiled at his lover. Ned could be such a drama queen. He held out his hand, waiting for the key.

"Ned, I'm sorry."

Ned, aesthete that he was, did something completely out of character. He grabbed Stone by the shoulders, spun him around, and smashed him against the door.

"You aren't sorry, you're sick." His eyes were ice. "You're going to fuck up every meaningful relationship over your mother. You disgust me. Kamela was right. Norman Bates, revisited."

Stone was shocked. He sputtered out, "But you don't understand—"

"I understand perfectly. She lives in you, and she'll never leave you. Never. And I'm not going to be your goddamned exorcist. You're pretty cute for a budding psychopath; too cute. That's dangerous for me. My self-destruction is merely an affectation; I want to keep it that way."

"You can't mean this—"

"—is what I've been saying to myself all week: he's not talking to me because I don't hate his mother. Howie, I don't share your obsession with her. Paint a picture, get it out of your system. Now shut up. I want to remember you."

He embraced Stone in his pale arms and gave him a kiss, full on the lips. The kiss ended in a sharp, stinging bite. Stone jumped back, surprised. Ned looked like a vampire, all in black, a dot of blood on his lips.

"They say you can't get blood from a Stone." He laughed at his own joke. "Oh, well. The key, Howard. There's only room for one nut in this relationship, dear. And you've upstaged me."

You took that away from me, too. Stone shivered next to the station wagon. Ned had earned quite a bit of notoriety. He lived in London now, owned and operated a graphic design company that designed book jackets and CD booklets for arty authors and pop bands. He'd also written and illustrated an award-winning children's book. Stone never heard from him or Kamela.

He had a sudden urge to burn the boxes of the crap he was bringing up, to destroy them in a raging bonfire. But he stopped himself. After closing the car door, he went in the house to get himself a glass of water. On his way to the kitchen, he saw her. A holographic ur-Madonna. She even seemed to move. He felt her spirit hovering everywhere: in the house, in these magazines and books, in this car. She did live inside of him and popped into memories like an uninvited guest. Even his very soul was her domain. How to be rid of her? The violence he'd felt earlier returned. He wanted to shred the wallpaper from the walls, rip the stuffing out of the couches. To shatter the haunted picture. He stopped himself. The violence he felt wasn't physical, it was spiritual and he had to battle her encroaching presence on a spiritual level. But how?

The Emerald City Bar was dank and smoky, just as he'd thought it would be. The low level lighting hid the dark green of the decor—the bar stools and the green marble countertop. In the other room, there was loud music and dancing; flashing lights changing colors. Stone sat rigid, as he nursed a Tom Collins through a thin green straw. He scanned the prowling, roving males. Maybe this wasn't such a good idea; he suddenly felt his age. The blaring, computer-chip pop bands gave him a headache. He just couldn't get into the bleeping, oddly rhythmic music—the DJ announced, "Here's 'Ventolin' by Aphex Twin." A thousand boys gave themselves to the swooshing music, a bacchanalia. One boy in chaps walked through the audience, fording his way through. Stone fixated on his glistening, pale buttocks.

He'd misjudged. Stone heard the name The Emerald City and immediately thought of old school queers: Judy Garland queens; a piano playing show-tunes. But this was too modern. After he finished his drink, he would try another bar.

A human voice accompanied by acoustic guitar and muted orchestration broke the monotony of dance music. The voice was female, both smoky and crystalline, like a cross between Enya and Billie Holiday. Stone glanced up to the small monitor above the bar. For once, a video that didn't make his head throb. The singer was dark, coffee-colored, and she wore an electric-blue sari. She was Asian, though her music was a mixture of blues and classical. The video intercut sinuous images of her against a background of shifting, silvery fonts—the lyrics, apparently—with a narrative. A young boy was sneaking around in a dilapidated mansion, trying door after door. The effect was hypnotic. At the song's climax, the final door was flung open and the boy's horrified face gazed upon the embalmed corpse of some huge Eva Peron-like figure, on a dais, surrounded by wax orchids and cheap votive candles. Weird, but effective. The credits flashed on the screen: "Sediment" by Ganesa, dir. Edward Meniscus.

It was several moments before Stone put his drink down. Edward Meniscus: Ned. So, he'd turned to video direction as well. Bitterness and hatred rose in his throat. He slammed down money on the countertop and turned to stalk out of the bar. He stumbled into a dark man with a small mustache; he was reminiscent of Langston Hughes, features-wise. He didn't seem mad and smiled at Stone.

"I'm sorry," Stone said, slow and deliberately.

"Not at all," the man returned, "the fault was all mine."

The drive home had been long. Billboards and neon signs sped past, burst into flame. The giant pig in front of the Piggly Wiggly Supermarket glared at him, like one of Ned's drawings. He'd been inattentive during his conversation with Brion. But the bits and pieces he'd heard—the man did Patti LaBelle and Dorothy Dandridge in a weekend drag show—was enough to convince him that he'd made the right decision. When they got to the house, Brion insisted on a nightcap before retiring. He passed by her.

"Who's this?" Brion asked, sipping a gin and tonic.

"My mother."

"She still lives here?"

Stone almost said yes. "Sometimes."

Brion looked confused by the statement. "You have her eyes."

"No, I don't. Finish your drink."

Stone began to knead Brion's shoulders. He was awkward; it had been too many years. He then steered him upstairs, leading to the Forbidden Room. Its guardian angel, in a tube top and stretch pants, with the wings of a Llardro figurine, said, Don't.

"Shut up," said Stone.

"Excuse me?" said Brion.

"Shut up," Stone said, and quieted him with a kiss. Oh, it had been too long. His mouth was sweet. His darkness was Kamela's, and his maleness was Ned's. Brion broke the kiss and glanced toward the bed, huge and foreboding. A horror movie bed. Some ancient Hollywood crone should be moldering away on that bed, Joan Crawford or Bette Davis.

"Are you sure we should do it here? I mean, it looks like an antique."

"It's fine," Stone said. "I've always wanted to do it in this bed. Get yourself comfortable. I'll be back."

Stone's erection was painful. But he had to complete the ceremony. He ran downstairs and pulled the portrait of Martha Stone from the wall. He walked up the stairs carefully. The room's guardian angel was smoking a cigarette; she wore a green polyester leisure suit and scowled at him. He pushed her out of the way. He propped the portrait on top of a drawer chest facing the bed. The lace curtains were pulled, a dark form stirred within. The next thing he knew, Stone was in the bed, writhing and wrestling.

You there, Mother? See me? I'm having sex with a Negro man. Look at me. Watch me.

I can't, Howard. The curtains are closed.

"So they are. Just a second."

"What?" Brion murmured.

Stone pulled himself off of Brion and opened the curtains. There she was, a head floating about the chest.

"What's that?" Brion lifted himself up a little.

"Don't you worry about that—"

But Brion had seen. He began to laugh. Stone attacked him then. Within seconds, he had the man beneath him, moaning and laughing. The laughs became gasps. At the moment of climax, Stone shouted, "Look at me! Mother, look at me!" Something cracked. The bed shuddered with their orgasms. It shuddered with their weight. With a sickening jolt, they descended to the floor, riding a raft of white lace. When they realized they wasn't dead, or even hurt, Stone laughed triumphantly.

Brion extracted himself. "You are one sick child."

"Get out. I'll call you a cab, and pay them. But get out."

He gathered himself from the wreckage of the bed. As he walked out of the room, he glanced at his mother. The glass was cracked over her face. And she was dead. Dead.

He slowly became aware of knocking on his door. He withdrew from the landscape in front of him. This one was his best yet: spiny leaves strangled a noble dogwood tree; it wept petals; a Southern Belle knelt at the feet of a modern black woman in a business suit; Tara burned in magenta and gold flames. He put down his paintbrush. A bit histrionic, but it captured what he was trying to say.

Again the soft, insistent knocking. Who'd knock, when there was a doorbell? One of her stupid, redneck friends? Three weeks since she'd been exorcized and he still felt still euphoric. He walked up the stairs, and at the top was greeted by the face of a woman who had a magical grace. *Hello, Frida*. But Frida Kahlo didn't smile back, not like she would've. Frida didn't smirk or judge.

The living room was a mess. He could scarcely remember ripping up his work for the greeting card company. Now the mangled cheap imitations of Beatrix Potter artwork littered the floor like confetti He stepped over these and a couple empty cobalt-blue vodka bottles. He was an artist; he was entitled to moods. And after a decade of restraint, why not kick up his heels a little?

The idiot knocked again. He smiled as he opened the door.

Mother stood there, wearing a flowering monstrosity of a hat: plastic pansies in dull colors. She was in a black gown (polyester, of course), one that trailed and draped over the front porch. One hand held a glass of Electric Lemonade. She'd had her hair freshly dyed, too, for this visit. The wax lily was still pinned to her gown as a poor debutante's cortège.

"Really, Howard," she said, pausing to sip her bright, urine colored beverage, "you didn't have to go that far to get my attention. Sleeping in my bed with a colored boy—as if I didn't know you was a bio-sexual. But my priceless bed—I could just cry, landsakes. Honestly! But don't you worry, dumplin', Mama was here last time you had one of your spells. She'll be here for this one. Now, I simply must do something about this pigsty." She kissed him, and enveloped him in her cloying, yet comforting fragrance. She floated into the room and at once began to tidy everything up.

There was a faint numbness on his cheek where she had kissed him. He put his hand there, pulled it away, and examined it. There was no blood. Just the coldness of the grave. Then he remembered. You can't get blood from a Stone. He laughed finally, at Ned's awful pun, feeling a peculiar kind of joy.

Come Join We

After my fever broke, I found that I could see things in a different way. People, animals, even some objects acquired a strange luminosity, as if seen through a prism. My grandmother's head, for instance, was swathed in a shimmering halo of pearly mist. At first I thought that this was only a trick of sight. I'd been sick for over two weeks; by then I was used to seeing things through a haze. Not only that, but my grandmother's hair was pearl gray. Maybe my eyesight had been damaged from the illness. I could accept this, but at times her head seemed to floating on a cloud of mist over her body. I would stare at what resembled flower petals in the mist, which always subsided, shrinking into an aura of dull silver around her head.

Granny's face would wrinkle with concern, like an old leather purse. I'd say nothing, keeping my miraculous vision to myself.

My mother's halo, on the other hand, would fluctuate between falling snow and silver glitter. It changed according to her mood like the holographic postcards of the Virgin the Sisters sold at the Divine Annunciation gift shop where she worked. Mary sorrowful, hands folded, eyes downcast; turned another way and you see Mary smiling, her eyes looking toward heaven.

But I could not ignore a stranger, a woman in our front doorway. And so I told Granny.

She adjusted her spectacles. She'd been working on her needlepoint. In turning her head, the shawl draped around her shoulders slipped. She peered at the doorway. She squinted.

"There's no such thing," she said. The mist around her French-braids subsided.

"Yes, there is." I was shivering. I was still weak. She walked over to me, and sat beside me on the sofa. She pulled my head to her bosom and enveloped me in cinnamon, rose toilet water and sweat.

"She still there?" she asked after a while.

I peeked through the mesh of her shawl. "Yes."

Granny looked through the mesh of the screen door. She said, in a theatrical tone of voice, "Go away, woman, and leave my grandson alone."

"Granny!" I said.

"I'm sorry. I just thought that... I'm sorry. What does she look like, this woman?"

I lowered the shawl. I felt safe in the circle of her arms yet I hesitated before describing her: "She's almost as tall as Mom, and a little darker than her, too. She's wearing a white dress with blue flowers printed on it. Her hair's braided and the braids are covered in glass beads. She looks so sad. She's crying."

The woman had begun floating on a blue-green mist, but I didn't tell Granny this.

Granny stopped holding me. Her eyes were unfocused, slightly glazed over. I snuggled against her for warmth, more out of habit than out of real fear. I knew that the woman in the doorway couldn't come inside. And if she did, she wouldn't hurt me.

Granny looked at the screen door with a suspicious eye. "White dress with blue flowers, eh?"

I nodded, burrowing into her bosom.

"Does she have a thin face, this woman you see?"

I stole a glance. "Yes—and there's a little spot of white, just above her right eye."

"Does she look like your mother?"

I nodded again.

Granny leaned back against the headboard. She gently pulled me against her. "It's your Aunt Ondine, who died before you were born."

"My Aunt Ondine?" I asked. I'd never heard of her before.

"Yes. She died fifteen years ago. She drowned."

I pulled myself out of Granny's grasp to study the woman. She wasn't looking at me, or anything at all, really. She seemed locked in her private world. If I stared at her too hard, she wavered. Ondine was pretty, with dark brown skin bathed in dew. Her eyes were dark and deep, gateways to something secret. Her tears had glints of iridescence in them. If anything, death made her beautiful not like those cinema films where ghosts were evil things, with worms in their eyes, reeking of the grave. I caught her scent. She smelled slightly of...oranges.

"How did she die?"

"I don't know if I should tell you," Granny said, standing up. "Your mother wouldn't like it."

I must have looked sad, or scared. Probably both. Granny relented. As she started on her tale, I kept a close eye on Aunt Ondine.

"Ondine was my first girl child, she came on the heels of your Uncle Zeke. It was a difficult birth. Three days of sweating and pain. And what did I get for all that work? A fragile thing, not much larger than your Granddad's hand. She came feet first. I should have known, then. She didn't seem to like life much. Like she knew that her time here was limited. She was a sweet, dreaming girl child, her thoughts turned towards other things. At first, I thought she was a mute, 'cause she didn't say nary a word. Maybe I was too busy having other kids, or taking care of your Granddad." Ondine was disappearing, her mist blending into the overall blueness of dusk. "Then one day, she's four or so, she says to me, 'Why is the sea whispering?' In just those words. I was just besides myself—"

"How come you didn't go to the doctor, to have her checked out?"

"In those days, we were a lot more isolated than we are now. They hadn't even built the bridge. People who wanted to see us took the ferry.

"So, anyway, I say to Ondine, 'Why, dumplin, that's just the sound of the tide. And she looks at me, her face as solemn as a monk's. She says, 'No. I hear voices. People talking, whispering in the sea.' So I said to her—"

The screen door slammed open. Mom home from her job at the vendor-booth. She walked right through her now transparent sister. She walked over to me, and planted a kiss on my forehead. "Feeling better?"

"Yes."

Granny had gotten up, and was heading toward the kitchen.

Mom asked, "You feel good enough to go to school tomorrow?"

"Not that good."

She laughed. The tiredness vanished from her face momentarily.

I could see the crying woman no more.

I said to Mom, "Granny was just telling me about Ondine."

She frowned at me, then at grandmother. Strands of cloud-snow engulfed her aura. She was angry.

"What did you tell him that for?"

Granny was quick and sly: "The child had been rifling through some old photograph books. He came upon her picture. What's so wrong about telling about your sister?"

Mom had no answer for that. Her snow-flare darkened and swirled.

"I think that the child ought to know about his family's history." Granny looked away from her daughter and pretended to be annoyed. I could tell that she was lying, her pearl-light pulsed triumphantly.

"Boy, what are you looking at?" My mother's voice was sharp.

"Nothing," I stuttered. I wrapped myself in a blanket.

Mom moved away, looking for dinner. Eventually, her snow settled down, becoming less fluttery. Only one more weird thing happened that night: when she sat down to pray, my mother's aura shimmered and snuffed out when she held her rosary. The rosary beads, heavy and lead, didn't jingle as they usually did. They hissed.

After a few days, I found that I could walk without stumbling, and keep solid food down. Mom sent me back to school. I walked there in the early morning, crunching through the soft gravel road. A recent storm had left the island's ground soggy and the air clear and moist. The road I took was parallel to the beach; between trees I caught glimpses of the shining ocean, and off in the distant, a greenish blur that was the coast of Georgia. A few black dots chugged and puffed in the middle of that expanse of water: the ferries to our island. I veered off the path, heading for wilder country. Soon I was nearing the top of a hill.

Spring was starting. I splashed through black puddles, thinking of the story of the Tar Baby.

It would be horrible to be stuck like that, in the ooze, but it would also be fun. I found that flowers, with my new sight, glowed even in the bright sunlight. They didn't have auras; their radiance was contained within.

At the top of the hill, I came upon a small, brown hare sitting up on its hind legs, its nose twitching, in front of a bluebell. At once I was enveloped by an overpowering fragrance. The cloy of sweetness, the moist of earth, the clear of water all rushed at me, making me drunk. The blue of the flower was more, somehow. Violet embers, stroke of pollen—I sat down, dizzy. I found that I knew everything about the hare. Its home, hidden deep within a briar patch, constantly evading foxes. I knew the story told by clay, mud, and tar. I closed my eyes, trying to distance myself from our brotherhood, the rabbit and I.

When the nausea subsided, I opened my eyes cautiously. He was gone. But I wasn't alone. I saw an old woman staring at me intently. Her hair was long pearl gray, and contained in two braids. Her skin was wrinkled and red, like clay. Her eyes were warm, dark and familiar. She wore trousers and simple blouse. I could tell by her wavering that she was dead—like Aunt Ondine. I wasn't afraid of her, though. I'm not sure why.

She walked over to me, and sat down.

Are you all right? she asked. She didn't move her lips, or even smile. In spite of that she seemed friendly.

"Yes," I said.

She put an arm around me. I could feel it. Her touch was feathery.

"Who are you?" I asked after a while.

She just glanced at me and smiled.

Ask your grandmother.

Her smile dazzled me like a prize, a flash of teeth like cowry shells. The wrinkles around her mouth and eyes were tiny canyons, pressed into the folds of her skin.

She tapped me on the shoulder. Look.

I turned around, following her pointing finger. There, on the beach below us, were hundreds of wavering people, both red and brown. They wore a mishmash of old fashioned clothes. Black folk wore bright, if clean, rags—homespun dresses and kerchiefs for the women, gray suits for the men. Indians (they could be nothing else) wore everything from leather to linen, and all points in between. They walked hand in hand, mixing with one another. A fire burned on the beach, even though this was early morning. Trays of corn, beef, chicken, greens and other things waited cooking. My mouth watered. I'd only eaten a thin, watery bowl of farina that morning. Two people on the beach spotted us, a tall, thin Indian woman in flowing robe with a stylized design on it, and her boyfriend, a young black man, the same color as me, in a white suit.

We waved back, the old woman and I. Then I felt incredibly sad. For I learned their story. The old woman showed me it, without words. Years ago, they'd escaped from slavery. The scent of sugar, the damp of the rice fields, the sting of cotton was on their hands, shimmering in their haloes. Some people in the group were clearly damaged. Welts and scars decorated their bodies. There was a man with half an ear. I saw a woman with roughened, pockmarked skin—she'd been burned. I could hear them singing now: plaintive gospel voices intertwining with majestic chants. Two kinds of "savagery", as my mother would call them, mixing. I heard that savagery, of their pride. Even in death they wore it. The man with half an ear was transformed by it. His lost ear became a whole black shell, inlaid with mother-of-pearl. The woman's burned face became a sculpture's head, carved of rock. People's scars became maps of pain and survival. I heard the savage pride in their music, too, in drums from Africa, from old America. Weaving together until—

I bent over and retched. Farina burned my throat. I saw the peaceful village wiped out. Men, on horses, carrying torches. The crack of gunfire and bones. The whole village wiped from the beaches. In an instant I saw blackened and reddened bodies, lying side by side. I saw the bodies sinking beneath the sand.

I turned to the old woman sitting next me.

"Why did you show me this?" I croaked out.

She said nothing. She smiled. It was a horrible thing, that smile.

I went back home, in a daze. Granny greeted me, surprised. She felt my forehead, and immediately sent me to bed.

A few hours later, she came in, bringing a bowl of soup with her. I told her about my encounter with the woman, but not about the massacre. I didn't want her to worry too much.

"This woman," Granny said, "she was red, like clay?"

"Yes."

"And when she smiled, her teeth were uneven, but the whitest teeth you ever saw?"

"Yes."

She sat still, considering something or other. She was smoking her pipe. A rich, pungent smell of tobacco rose.

"That was my Aunt Zora. Your great, great aunt. She was half Algonquian, and crazy as a loon. So my parents thought. But I loved her, when I was a child. She would sing to me, Indian songs about corn, birds, and such." She paused, the wrinkles in her face cracking with concentration. "I can't remember them. They're gone."

A melody snaked its way into my head. It was one of the songs from the scene on the beach. I sang it to my grandmother. She smiled, her whole face did. "That's it, child, that's it! One of the songs. You have the gift. Like I reckon Zora and Ondine did. Zora would always be talking about voices. She'd always be talking about hearing people singing."

Granny looked off into the distance, seeing beyond my bedroom wall. "Or screaming." Her aura deepened in color. It took on a bluish tint. If pearls were blue, they'd be that color.

"What's wrong?" I asked her.

"Ondine heard voices in the swamp, that called to her." Granny got up, and began to clear away the dishes. She pulled the shawl tight around her shoulders.

"Aren't you gonna tell me what happened to her?"

Granny didn't look at me. "You need to get your rest. Go to sleep, child, so you'll get better."

She closed the door on me, leaving me with memories that wasn't my own.

When I got better I went back to school. By now I could pretty much ignore my heightened senses. It helped that I was considered to be kind of odd by my classmates anyway. So when I saw that their auras were bright orange or urine-yellow, and giggled, they paid me no mind. Besides in the daytime, these things wasn't as clear as they could be.

One day in Sister Margaret's math class, I was drifting between protractors, proofs and equations. I found that the room was multifaceted, and upside down. I felt everything—the slightest breeze, a classmate's sneeze, and the vibration of Sister Margaret's chalk on the board—throughout my body. The trick was to weave my fibrous, filament-nerve in one corner, hidden. Then I'd wait for the violet-silver shimmer of dinner's wings. I folded my legs into myself.

"Aime," said Sister Margaret, in her habit of fly-black and soft underbelly white. "I asked you a question. Describe to me what an isosceles triangle looks like."

I cried out.

My classmates giggled nervously. Sister Margaret frowned. Then she followed my gaze, up to where my eyes rested. In the corner of the chalkboard, rested a black spider, nestling in a spool of gossamer. Sister Margaret and many of the girls in the room screamed. Except for Gwen, who stood up and captured the spider. She was fearless. She placed Brother Spider in front of me, stepping gingerly to my desk. She put it on my prayer book. I smiled at him, having heard his story. I admired his cunning, trapping the insects in his masterpiece of a home.

Sister Margaret bought her answer book down on the spider. I screamed. A thousand eyes closed forever.

"Aime, what are you yelling for?" she asked him. Her face was a mask of disgust, as she lifted her sticky book back up.

"You are a murderer!" I cried.

Her disgust dropped, briefly. Her aura flamed. She loved control.

"What do you mean, boy, that I am a murderer?"

"You killed him— "

Her eyes narrowed. "For killing a small, foul insect, you think that I am a murderer? Aime, go to Father John."

"What for?" I don't know what possessed me. I wasn't usually this forceful. "You're the one who killed an innocent soul, who could teach you more about geometry—"

"Aime. I will say this once: go to Father John."

I left the classroom, accompanied by my classmates' chorus of ohhhs and ahhhs. As I went down the hall, I thought to myself, What just happened? The new way of seeing things didn't bother me so much. I was more concerned with the how of my new powers of observation. I didn't remember the exact time of my illness. When I remembered the day that I became ill, all I could see, in my mind, was the forest on the North side of the island. Up in the trees, I saw row upon row of moth egg sacs, oozing and webbed.

I shook that image out of my head as I went to Father John's office, with the note that Sister Margaret had given me. After he read it, he questioned me about my actions. I confirmed them. He took out a stiff, leather strap, and asked me to put my hand out across the desk. I complied, knowing what to expect.

Crack! Crack! Crack! went the strap across my tender palm. But I didn't feel it. I was entranced by Father John's halo. It glowed dark and murky. It was tarnished, not at all like the circles of gold around Jesus and Mary's heads.

I began to find that my strange vision was more of a nuisance than a miracle.

One day in Social Studies, Sister Ernestine was teaching us about the Father of Our Country. I drifted in the class usually because of her bewitching beauty. She was the youngest of the sisters, and her skin was smooth and brown like a chocolate milkshake where the other Sisters' were cracked and parched like the earth in drought-times. She had large, doe-like brown eyes and the most striking lips: the top one was dark and smooth, like her skin, and the bottom lip was flamingo-pink.

My history book was lying open, and my elbows rested on either side of it. I wasn't really listening to Sister Ernestine; I was following her with my eyes. I noticed the swellings and movements of her form beneath her habit, the way her wimple left an exposed patch of her soft hair. And her aura—it got me in trouble.

She called on me, while I was dreaming of saving her from some villain. I didn't know what the question had been; I was just thrilled that she had asked me something.

I said to her, dreamily, "You're glowing, like the pink part of a conch shell."

Sister Ernestine looked at me blankly. Then she blushed, her ears turning purple. Her aura turned that color, too, more or less.

The boys in the row behind me snickered. That seemed to set her off. She ran out of the room, tears flowing down her face. The class didn't know what to do. We had never seen teachers behave in this way. We were used to cruelty. Minutes passed in silence. After a while, someone, I think it was Gwen, made a half-hearted attempt at tomfoolery. Even she, who was usually fearless, was uncertain. It was almost relief we felt when Father John barged into the room. He stood there for a second, scanning the children's faces before he found the culprit. Me.

Then he marched over to me, and yanked me up. He grabbed my arms, squeezing hard. I wasn't hurt, though I should have been. I was too busy noticing that murky outline of his fingers on my flesh. Then BANG. Something hit my head, blanking out my vision. Then I felt the pain. A sharp object was wedged against my scalp. It was only when he released me, in his office, that I could see again in that strange way. I turned to regard Father John, in his dark clothing. The object banging against my head had been his crucifix.

He forced me to sit down, and called my mother at the gift shop. In about ten minutes, she arrived, flustered and out of breath.

"Father... John... I... came... here—"

"Please have a seat, Rebekiah."

My mother sat. She still wore her uniform. As she gained her breath, she glared at me. Snow, this time. A blizzard.

"Tell me what this is about."

Father John sat at his desk, arranging himself in an actorly way. "It seems that your son has taken an active interest in vulgarity."

"What do you mean?"

Father John repeated what I said to Sister Ernestine, changing my words.

Mom looked at me, on the verge of tears, or murder.

I said, "But--"

"Child!" they both said in unison. Mom finished the sentence: "Speak when you are spoken to."

I ignored them: "But that's not what I said. I like Sister Ernestine. I told her that she glowed pink, like a *conch* shell."

Both of them looked at me coldly. Apparently this wasn't much better than what they thought I said.

In the end, it was Mom that got me out of serious trouble. She explained to Father John that I had been sick for a long while, and perhaps this was just an after-effect of the illness... When I got home, she gave me a spanking, and sent me to bed, without supper.

This vision thing was quite annoying.

For weeks afterward, when I went in public, I wore my mother's rosary beads underneath my shirt. They hid, if only partially, the worst of the visions. I caught glimmers here and there of the outrageous stuff, and the auras sank down into nothingness. For weeks, I was free of plaguing images. I felt safe and normal once more with the cold lead beads against my skin. Every now and then, and in the evenings before Mom came home, I took them off. At once, I was pushed back into a multi-layered reality.

I took walks after my homework. In the forest, I could see the birds, insects, and flowers. Watching them glow, dart and radiate was my favorite thing to do in the evenings. Once, I saw Ondine, in her white dress with blue flowers, silently following Granny on her way to the grocery store. She caught sight of me, and waved. I was hesitant to wave back. Part of me wanted to talk to her, to have her tell me her story. But somehow, I knew that in her spirit state, she wouldn't speak. What she had to tell me would be told in her graceful, balletic movements, and through images. All the same, I wasn't too keen on that method of storytelling. What Zora had shown me still scared me. I viewed my sight with ambivalence. And I avoided the hilltop and the beaches.

Sometimes, after school, I would wait for Mom on the park bench just opposite the cathedral. I'd watch tourists and visitors from the mainland drift by. It was better than kaleidoscopes, watching their auras mingle and blend with one another.

One day, I was doing just this, when someone sat next to me. I didn't notice anyone until a voice said, "What are you doing, Boy?"

I turned and saw this man, nearly seven feet tall and black as molasses. He wavered. His hands were large, the fingers splaying off his hands like roots. Even the palms of his hands were dark. I looked into his eyes, seeing that they held things. A memory of openness and wideness. I scaled mountains with him and ran the plains. I also knew confinement, chains, and the smell of my neighbors above and below me. I stalked a sea hungry with sharks and floating bodies—

I looked away from his eyes. They were worse than what Zora had shown me. I focused on his root-hands and beet-purple clothes.

How you like seein' things?. His voice boomed and gonged in my mind,

"Not much," I told him. "It gets me into trouble."

It can do that, certainly. And he laughed, a deep, woody chuckle. I could feel plates beneath the earth move. After a while, even watching his spectral fabric became disturbing.

I cut to the chase: "Who are you? Are you one of my relatives, here to show me some awful thing? If you are, I don't want to see it!"

He laughed again. I felt thunder and waterfalls, this time. It was a laughter that was bitter and innocent at once.

I am your relative, and everyone else's.

"What do you mean by that?"

The giant root-man stood. His purple and magenta surged and swirled. *I have many names. Ask your Granny who I am.*

"No thank you." I was petulant.

He was well over seven feet now; I reached his shin.

That is fine, for now. We'll have all of forever, after you come join we.

He threw his huge head back, and roared with laughter. Then he dispersed.

"Aime!" Mom's shrill voice carried across the park. "Who were you talking to?"

"No-one," I told her. I walked home sullenly.

"You were talking aloud," she said. I looked up at her. There was concern in her voice.

I got out of my sulking. "It was just an imaginary playmate."

"You sure?"

"Yes, Mom, I'm sure."

I didn't tell Granny about the giant. This aspect of my sight, I wanted to go away. The dead always had sad stories to tell. However, I knew that this giant was no mere dead thing. He was something more. Something even more terrible than a recording of death.

Things got worse. One day in music class, the rosary beads warm against my skin, I began to see spirits tramping in and out of the classroom. We were learning Ave Maria, wobbly children's voices just slightly out of tune. I was playing the melody on a glockenspiel. Sister Agnes was leading us, with bold, exaggerated strokes of her wand. The dead gathered around her. Angels in robes of blue, their haloes gold. Or maybe they wore wreaths, made of holly, flowers and candles on their heads, and sashes made of Christmas tree lights, their wings of aloe leaves. They began to sing with us, eventually drowning us out.

"Aime," said Sister Agnes, "pay attention."

I found it impossible to do so.

I realized the rosary beads no longer worked. Instead of hiding the spirit world, they now intensified it.

I suffered through these visitations in earnest, though. My mother grew more concerned, and my grandmother grew more distant. I longed to tell them that no, I wouldn't go mad, like Aunt Zora, or follow swamp-voices, like Ondine. But I couldn't give them that assurance. I was unsure myself.

On Easter Sunday, I was forced into a stifling suit. Mom wore a bright floral print and a wide, black hat with a veil. Granny wore a royal blue dress, and a hat festering with plastic flowers. We walked down the main street. Granny and Mom complimented the other grownups. I just noticed the other kids, uncomfortable, squirming. When we got to Divine Annunciation, we all forgot our glamour and our discomfort. It was beautifully decorated. Large Easter lilies framed each pew. Candles writhed and flickered on the stage, even though it was daylight. Fresh cut tea roses surrounded the statue of Jesus, and votive candles encircled the image of Mary. I was impressed, for about two minutes. Then I sat down on the hard pew with my legs dangling.

Father Anthony began his sermon, droning about this or the other. I drifted.

At first, I thought there were some children whispering somewhere in the audience. I scanned around for them. Mom popped me on the thigh. "Sit still," she hissed. I still heard the whispering; she didn't. I knew it was the spirits. Maybe I can ignore them this time, I thought. But then everything flared; people's auras were like the neon signs I saw when I visited the mainland. Everyone's head glowed. The voices became more sibilant, and harsher. I put my hands over my ears, to drown them out. It was no use. I heard them in my head. "Stop that!" Mom slapped my thigh again. The white stone beams of the church began to move with vines. Like snakes, jungle vines began to creep up the sides of the church. Did no one else see this?

Suddenly, the wavering spirits began to crowd into the church, a singing throng of black and red folk, festooned with the jewelry of death. They drowned out the priest's droning lecture. The statue of Mary moved, surging with energy. She stood up from her cage of votive candles. She shed her white lady form, and changed into something fluid and ancient. Dark, flat head, and canary yellow skirt, topless, her breasts drooping. Jesus did that same thing. He broke away from his cross, and his skin turned red. His hair was lusterless black and hanging down his back. He didn't smile. He wore war paint. Both of these figures advanced on me slowly, as the church drowned in vines, and took on the color of seawater, swamp water. I made to stand up. At either end of the pews, stood Zora and Ondine. I could not escape. I screamed.

I remember waking up in Father Anthony's office, on his sofa. Both my mother and he were talking. Granny was stroking my forehead.

Granny was saying, "He has the Sight. We have to save him, before he goes mad."

Mom was shaking, and crying. Father Anthony was consoling her.

I sat up, tentatively. They all looked in my direction.

I said, "I can't see anymore. Your sermon cured me. The church saved me."

Both Mom and Granny looked at each other. Their faces told a story.

"Granny, tell me what happened to Ondine," I said. It was summer dusk, muggy, and the cicadas were sizzling outside.

Granny put down her knitting. She was silent for a time, before she began. "She was seventeen, when she went to the swamp. I tried to stop her, many times before.

"'But they're singing to me, telling me to join them,' she told me. I never knew who they were."

Granny said nothing more than that. She went back to her knitting.

I could have told her who they were. But I didn't think that she would really appreciate it. Knowing myself was enough. Every now and then, I could hear their drums, their songs of sorrow, and joy. I could catch the rustle of their forms. I knew that I would join them, eventually. Not yet.

I watched as my grandmother's mist turned pearly-blue.

Sea, Swallow Me

The island hated him.

Jed could feel it as he walked down the empty street. A ghost town spread out before him. Houses with rickety, water-eaten planks and warped shingles, with broken glass or torn plastic where windows were. The street was covered with sand, jeweled with glass. The metal of a derelict car glinted in the heat. Was there electricity in these houses? Running water?

A Doberman lunged against an unstable fence, the barks of rage as sudden and relentless as machine gun fire. Jed jumped back, startled. He saw the tan underside of the dog, lewd with dangling genitalia. He laughed, out of fear or embarrassment.

The guidebooks had specifically warned tourists to avoid this section of town of La Mer Vert, unofficially called La Merde, a shantytown, with houses in ill repair, patched with corrugated tin. He felt sullen eyes on him. They hid in the shade of the silent houses. Jed shivered, in spite of the heat. Was the search for local color worth this feeling? This morning, he'd woken up in his hotel room. A gentle zephyr stirred the filmy curtains. The walls of the room were nautilus pink and touched with painterly strokes of morning sunlight. The generic painting above his bed showed a riotous marketplace scene. He heard gulls, children, and steel drums. It was horrible. The resort feel was starting to grate on him. Jed liked his vacation with a little bit of bite. One more fruit-filled, alcoholic drink, and he'd puke. But now that he was here, in La Merde, and having second thoughts. If he were killed here, who would find him? The killers would probably just throw him in the sea, to be nibbled by fish and covered by algae.

The street ended abruptly, quashing his morbid thoughts. There was a cul de sac, and then the beach. The scene took his breath away. Hidden behind this raggedy, dangerous street was one of the most beautiful beaches he'd ever seen. The sand was white and soft as powdered sugar. Off to the left, dunes undulated, with thin fingers of grass poking out of them. The ocean water was like a liquid geode. Smashed sapphire was shot through with veins of emerald and milky opal. The horizon was empty, no cirrus, no birds, just endless blue. Jed kicked off his sandals, and stepped onto the sand, entranced. The glimmering water beckoned. Salt air tickled his nose. Why does it glow like that? he thought. As if there was a sun under the water. When he reached the wet lip of land where the tide kissed it, he looked down. The water was clear and colored simultaneously. Something burned under his breastbone. It was joy, bright as the phantom sun under the water. He'd made the right decision coming here.

Jed stepped in the water, which was mercifully warm. He waded out, until the tide licked his knees. He saw shells and sand dollars in the silt floor. The wet sand oozed between his toes, holding him there. He closed his eyes. I am the only imperfect thing here. But that didn't matter. He wanted to forget the keloid's raised continent on his face, and his ashy skin and too-thin body. If he could only be like this forever.

He stood there for a while, and lost track of time. He wasn't really sure when he first heard the singing. It seemed to evolve out of the breeze and the sighing surf. Voices, soft and vaporous as sea mist, rose near him, and moved away. He turned away from the horizon, blue upon green-blue, and faced the shore. White and blue and black moved further away from him, a singing congregation of men and women. They wore linen suits and dresses, all of them blindingly white. The women looked clean, their brown skins gleaming. They had navy blue headscarves. The crowd moved in nimble, ghost-like steps down the beach. They ignored him; he was irrelevant. He might have been a rock in the sea, or a discarded buoy. Dark children wove in and out of the group of sixty, with orderly, mannered chaos. At the back, men dragged wagons filled with all sorts of things: white flowers, bottles with sheets of paper stuffed inside, perfect shells, and food. The chorus was steady, with the men's voices keening, and the women's voices reedy. Jed couldn't understand the language they were singing in. St. Sebastian had a notoriously difficult pidgin, archaic English mixed with colonial French and seasoned with an accent that had no precedent. He followed their subdued yet joyful progress down the white beach.

Back home in D.C., he'd witnessed an Easter parade held by the Ethiopian congregation that worshipped in the church behind his basement apartment. They marched down the alley like this group, led by priests that looked like life-sized black chess pieces. He recalled the decorated umbrellas, palm leaves and vibrant clothing—it was very much like this current group. But there was different feeling, here. The Ethiopians had shared a communal happiness; it was very much a celebration. These people in blue and white were becalmed, as if they were under a spell. They marched and sang toward the inevitable, rather than towards salvation and reward. It was eerie.

Maybe I'm reading too much into this. He moved out of the water, and followed them, at a discreet distance. Curiosity got the better of him. No one looked around; they all faced forward, even the children. The one baby, facing backwards and resting on his mother's shoulder, was sound asleep. They walked adjacent to the shoreline, and scarcely seemed to notice it. Every now and then, Jed would look to the Atlantic, and notice a change. Silver water became blue, then brown then green. Once, he saw the grey-silver flash of a pod of porpoises, arcing in the water. Another time, a bird of prey hovered. Every time he paused to look seaward, he found that the group had moved further ahead than he thought possible. Oddly enough, he could hear their voices all the same—their sound did not diminish. After the fourth time distracted by the activity on the water, he resolved to follow them, and ignore the periphery.

Jed settled into their gait. He focused on their linen-covered backs, and their dark necks. The women's hips swiveled and bopped. They were rounded, and breasts were full. They were totemic, living sculptures, Black Madonnas. A few of the men were shirtless, with firmly muscled backs and buttocks that slid underneath pants with ease and grace. Stomp, sway, sing—Jed found himself singing their song, even though he didn't understand the words. The melody just got into his blood, like an infection.

Finally, they stopped. Jed stopped as well, wishing that there was a dune or something that he could hide behind. They seemed intent on what they were doing; maybe they wouldn't notice him blatantly looking at them. Still, he felt like he was invading their privacy. Even so, he felt no strong urge to move. Presently, the group formed a semi-circle, a crescent of blue, white and brown at the lip of the ocean. Their voices rose, and were accompanied by percussive instruments and handclaps. One by one, they reached into the laden wagon to their left, and dropped trinkets into the water. Bottles, beads, feathers, coins, and other things were laid out on the shoreline, and devoured by the incoming breakers. From where he stood, it looked like the offerings disappeared. He saw a wreath of flowers drift on the wrinkled surface of the water. They gleamed against the kaleidoscopic water as they floated slowly towards the horizon. Jed imagined one of the porpoises leaping through the hoop of white blossoms. After the last offering, the music stopped abruptly.

He heard the distant screech of seagulls. Then silence.

A figure in a long robe of blue stepped out of the crescent of gathered people, and stood facing them, its back to the water. The being was long limbed with hair cut close to its skull. It was male, but so old that the masculine features had eroded like stone. A priest beyond gender. It glanced over his flock, and saw Jed lurking. The ageless gaze captured him, held him momentarily, and released him. Jed's keloid itched and burned, perhaps irritated by the salt air.

The priest spoke to its congregation. The words flowed out like the tide. Its voice was musical and slightly feminine. The patois of St. Sebastian rippled over Jed's ears. He supposed it was a sermon of some kind. But who were these people worshipping? He remembered vague rumors of cults in the island, where people followed African rituals—the guidebook had mentioned obeah and Voudun. But this worship was swathed in mystery. The priest seemed little bothered by his presence. It stretched out its arms. In response, the audience began to chant and sing. They stood still—even the formerly restless children—and sang a simple song that increased in tempo and velocity slowly. Jed couldn't make out the whether it was in French or Spanish—or some older, pre-colonial tongue. The priest conducted them, as if they were instruments in an orchestra. One word was repeated, over and over. It rose and separated from the flow of voices: Olo Kun.

There was a magic about all words that began with the letter O. It was something that Jed had felt as a child when he was first learning to read. It was a silly thing, but the feeling never left him. Owl and opal and Orion were beautiful words. O was the letter that was an endless circle, that surrounded a hole. It was geometric and mysterious, mystical and mathematical, the cousin to 0, the number that signified nothing. He found himself saying the word with the group of worshippers.

The voices and their rhythms had insinuated themselves into him, into his blood:

Syllable, sibilance, Olokun...
Beat, beat, Olokun...

Sigh, bird's cry, Olokun...
Serpent words, serpent sun, Olokun...
Olokun... Olokun... Olokun.

The spaces between the magic word got smaller and smaller. Soon there was no word but Olokun. A word that meant everything. A word that meant sea and sky and sand. A word that was also a name, a name that meant endless and terrifying blue.

The name came faster and faster, darker and darker, cresting waves of human voices, voices of the congregation, of the bizarre priest(ess). Indeed, his voice mimicked the tug and pull of the surf and the darker currents. They stood on the lip of the ocean, calling for the he, or she, or it.

And It, or She, or He came.

O, or Zero, is magic, because it holds emptiness. It defines space, and captures it. What lives in the center of Zero, or O?

A woman broke free of the crescent of people (half an O). She was an explosion, given human form. She screamed, and her eyes rolled back into head. She staggered in paroxysm for a few steps, before she fell to the ground. She could have been something spit up by the sea. The semicircle dispersed.

It was second nature, really, him running down to where she had fallen. Last summer's stint as an EMT had prepared him for all sudden medical episodes. It was essential that he act, and soon. The first few moments of an accident were crucial. The audience had parted and let him through. He dropped to his knees, and reached for her slack arm that poked out of her robes' sleeve.

"Non," said a strange, high-pitched voice. Jed looked up, into the eyes of the priest. It towered over him. The priest's neck was impossibly long, and Jed noticed thick, yellow nails on its ancient, veiny hands. Its gaze was stern, and reminded Jed of a vulture, of the strange, feminine bird creatures from the movie *The Dark Crystal.*

"I am an EMT—a doctor," he said, even though it wasn't quite true. He wasn't a doctor yet. Med school started in the fall. "I can help."

The priest shook its head. "Non. You mustn't touch her. She not sick."

The woman's mouth was open. A pool of drool had formed in the corner of her lip. Her eyelids fluttered.

Jed repeated himself: "I can help her," and took her thin, brittle wrist in his hand.

He burned. His keloid flared and throbbed—an island of pain on the side of his face. He saw endless blue, cut through with emerald, the bottom of a boat, shoals of fish. He jumped back as if shocked. The inert woman jerked back to life. 10,000 volts thrummed through her invisibly. Her jaws quivered, and her eyes flew open. Jed was on the sand, rubbing his keloid. He saw for the briefest moment the woman's eyes.

They were blue, a rich, impossible color. She had no whites in her eyes—just twin ovals of blue. He saw movement in them—tiny daggers of sunlight. Or fish?

Before he could look further, she stood up. But *stood* implied a control of her body, the obeying of anatomy and physical reality. No, she did not stand. She sprung up with such exuberant fluidity, it was as if her bones were malleable as clay. She was a short woman, perhaps 5'4, and yet now she loomed over him. And it wasn't just that he was on the ground. Maybe the rest of the world shrank, in response to her.

The first spasm of her body had Jed scrambling off his ass. He moved back to join the circle that had formed around the woman. She began to shudder, as if she'd caught a sudden chill. And then, she started dancing, if such chaotic movement could be called dancing. It was simultaneously robotic and graceful.

The throng started chanting the name of the god again and again: *Olokun! Olokun! Olokun!* As before, he joined in with them. He felt the massed sound in his body, in his blood. The woman's wild dance sped up. Jed remembered seeing some program or another about krumping, a spastic, high-energy dance that was in the ghetto underground back home. Young men and women would hurl themselves into hiphop rhythms with abandon. Muscle and bone became water. It was similar to what he saw now. It was terrifying. She would hurt herself, if she didn't stop—

The vulture-priest emerged from the circle with slow, steady steps. The krumping dervish ignored it, entranced by the chanting crowd and her own hummingbird beats. The priest stood in front of her, and was spattered by her profuse sweat and droplets of spit.

It raised a hand. A sapphire ring glittered on one finger. The hand swooped down like a diving bird of prey. It smacked the center of her forehead.

She stopped moving at once.

The crowd stopped chanting.

The sigh of the sea filled in the sonic void.

"Speak!" commanded the priest.

The sea just sighed. And the woman began to reek. A smell came off her, of salt and stagnation, fish, seaweed and chemicals. She was a statue in white and blue. She suddenly moved. It was a lurch into motion. She jerked, as if she were flotsam and the sand was the sea. She shook her head vigorously, and beads of sweat flowed off her body. Her blue scarf came undone and undulated to the ground. A grove of black coral—her braided hair—fell around her shoulders. She opened her eyes:

Blue, fringed with the shawl of foam, no whites in the corners. She fixed her gaze on Jed. She advanced as slowly as a zombie. The surrounding crowd spread out away from him and her.

"You," she said, pointing a finger at him. Her voice was deep, thick and husky.

Jed's keloid tingled. It had risen from a cut he'd gotten when he was riding his bike to work a year ago. The ugly scar grew from the sea of his black skin. It was an island of deformity. For the past few months, he'd been able to ignore it. Now, it telegraphed every uncomfortable feeling he had. It was sensitive in the way arthritic bones were. Fear was the emotion that he felt. This woman was clearly deranged, and doubtlessly held some power over the gathered crowd. He felt completely the interloper, the American Black who might as well have been white. The eyeshaped portals to the sea captured his reflection. They mesmerized.

Jed broke eye contact, before he sank into them. He saw the priest at the periphery, where the white sand turned brown. He caught its eye: Help. The priest shrugged. He was beyond its power. He was in her hands now.

She repeated, "You," and her overwhelming smell hit him. She stepped right up to him, and got in his face. He felt small, even though he towered over her. She could crush him, if she wanted to. She did not. "You, you are mine."

Her voice was deep and male. A basso profoundo that creaked and cracked like hurricane-warped wood. She stank, and Jed thought of fishscales, wavering fronds, fishshit and oil. She smelled like leviathan whales, and the strange fish that dwell at the bottom of the ocean that have bioluminescence. "Mine…"

The sun at the bottom of the sea glowed. Dark blue into sapphire water.

All over the island, there were images of the patron saint. In churches, towel, t-shirt and grottoes. The fey youth pierced by arrows. Sebastian lent his name to hotels and clubs on the island. The Arrow Bed and Breakfast. Saint's Peak. The island's lone gay club was The Catamite. Those languorous eyes with luscious lashes, the slender youthful body, and the tortured pose were everywhere. You couldn't avoid them. Everywhere you turned, the murdered homosexual saint appeared, like Mary would in sandwiches and cloud formations.

The possessed woman's eyes pierced him with arrows tipped with toxins. The jolt of the eel and the sting of the ray were in that gaze.

"Mine…"

Echoes in underwater grottoes.

She took his hand, and Jed rose. He followed, wanting to hear the echoes. She pulled him to the water's edge, then into the water itself. They walked out into the water, which was as warm as mother's milk, knee high, then waist high. On the shore, the gathering had reformed their half-O shape. The woman, who was something more than a woman, led him on. Jed felt the silky carpet of the ocean floor. A smooth pebble or stone would graze his feet. Waves crested and they went underneath them for thrillingly brief seconds. He saw faces in algae, and fish made of sunlight. Before long, even that didn't matter. He floated, massaged by water streams. They stopped at some point, and just bobbed like buoys.

A current of cold water broke the spell, or whatever it was. The safety of the woman's grip ended. Jed felt the cold fingers of the current run through his legs. The cold bit him. They were frozen, and he began shivering immediately.

"What the hell…"

His guide was shocked awake with him. The sea spilled out of her eyes, into the surrounding water. She closed her eyes, and abruptly snapped awake, with prosaic brown eyes and panic in them. She shrieked.

"Calm down," Jed told her, through his chattering teeth. "We'll make it back to the shore together." There would be time later to figure out what had happened. The people on the shore were not quite dots. And the cold current wasn't that strong. He felt its insistent touch, as if he were being tickled by feathers of ice. His companion, completely freaked out by now, began to babble in her patios. She battled the waves, and began to swim, clumsily, toward the shore. Jed began to follow suit, and found that he couldn't feel his limbs. A lesson on hypothermia came back to him as he tried to control his cryogenic body. He felt the blood in his veins had turned to liquid nitrogen.

He watched as the woman made her slow progress to the shore, to the group of people who waited for her and loved her. He was frozen in the sea, a sacrifice to some unknown god. Jed strained his muscles, felt nothing. His body was no longer his own. Soon, he'd go into shock, and the gravity of the sea would pull him under. Surely, the people on the shore would realize what had happened to him, and would go for help? Unless this was his punishment for witnessing their secret service. Jed felt the stirrings of rage. Death was too big a penalty for seeing what was conducted in public. Those stupid savages… But, he remembered that they were kind, and had let him join in. He remembered clapping, and singing along with them. Of course, they would go for help, as soon as they realized what had happened to him. It would be too late to save him, though.

Almost as an afterthought, Jed called out. What started out as "help" turning in a long, anguished howl that was carried away by the wind, the sea, and various ambient noises. He tired his voice out. He drifted away, carried by a riptide. Rising hillocks of sapphire and emerald separated him from the shore.

"You are mine," the woman had said with the sea's voice. She was right; he was now of the water. Soon, he would be one with salt, and fish. Images and emotions of his past life flashed before his eyes in random and senseless order. Candy from a favorite aunt. Watching Prague emerge from the window of a train. The first time he had sex. He was giving all his memories—all of his essence—to the water. The sea had a name. Olokun.

Something within him, something dark and instinctual, reacted to the bubble of thought. The name meant something. Just thinking it made him less cold. Of course, he was going mad. But what harm to say the name aloud?

He managed "Olokun" as he sunk beneath a surge of saltwater. His lungs filled, then he popped back up like a buoy, and said the name again. His fingers tingled, as did the balls of his feet. He could feel his body again. He did not dare to hope what a third pronunciation might bring. Would he be free of the riptide? It was foolish, magical thinking, like the believers. And yet, Jed had never really been a committed agnostic. The supernatural was a nice idea; logic was overrated, as far as he was concerned. He said "Olokun" a third and final time.

The sea froze. Everything froze. No waves. No birds. No current. No sound. Jed might have been alone in the world. He saw each molecule of water. Beneath the water he saw a jellyfish, a translucent silver balloon with pastel organs, caught in the knot of time, as if trapped in blue Lucite. A spot of golden sunlight stained the surface of the sea. He could see the striations of wrinkles. The golden spot was an island of light on the face of the sea. The whole world held its breath. The arrow was knocked. Who did the world wait for?

Motion. It happened all it once. The crest of a wave, the shiver of jellyfish, a gulp of water in his lungs. The current came back, stronger than before, and it tugged him underneath the waves. He could no longer fight it. The sea swallowed him, pulled him down into the deep. Bubbles of air escaped him, little silver jellyfish heading for the surface that he would never see again. Cold water rushed to fill his lungs and nostrils, to crush them. He let out a gasp, to hurry the business of drowning. No bubble of air escaped.

Jed blinked. He took another breath, and found that his lungs were satisfied. The invisible current that he was trapped within was not cold, either. It was a warm as the zephyrs that played across St. Sebastian. He blinked, and found that he could breathe, even as the curtain-like drapes of sunlight slowly receded.

I am dead. Some chemical had dumped into his brain, and filled it with peaceful hallucinations to lead him to death, that was the only reasonable explanation. I might as well enjoy this elevator ride to Death.

He settled into the unseen cushion that bore him down in the yawning depths. The current led him through a shoal of grouper, with bright yellow fins and spotted like giraffes. They wove and danced around him, aquatic sunlight given form. Other, finer fish, in colors of green and electric blue appeared now and then, and ignored him. Jed flew past a coral bed, pink and treacherous. A shark lunged at him, but something—the current?—kept it at bay.

Down and down and down he went. A light disappeared; he found he could still see perfectly, as if he had dark-adapted eyes. He saw blue in the darkest tones, beyond the human spectrum. He made up names for the colors that he saw: Strata Blue. Stygian Cerulean.

Chthonian Indigo. He sped by valleys and chasms where who knew what lived. Giant squid, whales and other leviathans of the deep hid in the topography.

Just as Jed relaxed in the current, he noticed that the speed of his travel slowed the deeper he went. He looked behind him, since he was "seated" backwards, to see what new sights were ahead.

At first, he thought it was a cliff, a misshapen underwater mountain. Then he saw the "mountain" had familiar shapes in it. Car parts, pipes, coral, and shells, a mountain of junk. Engines and abandoned fans nested among coral reefs and various skeletons of long dead sea creatures. At various intervals were circular openings to the mountain; some of these were filled with the portal windows of ships. Fish darted out of the open ones, vanishing into the hollow center of the mountain, like tourists into a cathedral. With that thought, it occurred to him that this structure was, in fact, some kind of building. It was too arranged for it not to be. The current nudged him further on, to the bottom of the building of shells and sea wrecks. He stopped and hovered in the chthonian indigo, in front of a large door. It yawned. Its frame was formed by the ribs of some huge whale, and fringed with hundreds, thousands of glimmering coins—the long lost treasure of pirates. Irregular circles of gold, the embossing faded and verdigrised. Jed waited. The whole ocean floor waited.

For what?

For whom?

The answer was obvious. It vibrated in his heart, his head, and his soul. The excitement was inseparable from the fear. It thrummed through him, like electricity. He felt himself harden with anticipation.

In the hollow of dark contained by the steepled door, Jed saw movement—filmy, diaphanous swirls of movement. Cobalt dark changed to electric blue as the form resolved itself. The first thing Jed saw was the eyes. They burned, lambent and green like cat's eyes. But there was no oval slit to interrupt the green. It became clear that these glowing almond-shapes were eyes, when strange undersea light described a face. The skin was like lava turned to fabric. The high cheekbones and high forehead, the wide nose, the whole architecture of the face had some marvelous black stretched across it, hard as rock, and as soft as silk. Nappy, knotted hair adhered to the top of the head—black coral. As the figure emerged from the door, Jed saw the giant man's magnificent torso. Lava skin, firm pectorals, and the large dinner plate sized nipples, plummy in color. His waist tapered downward. Jed throbbed in anticipation—both his keloid and his groin. His eyes traveled down the molten skin, where surely perfectly shaped, large genitalia were.

Below the giant's waist was a finely woven garment of blue scales that shimmered with glints of green and gold. It was a skirt of peacock feathers. Jed looked for the garment's end, to see legs ropy and thick with muscle. He found that the garment continued, covering his feet, and ended with a filmy, flowing fin. Jed laughed— he could imagine the Icelandic singer Björk wearing such an outfit. Then realization struck with the force of a tidal wave. The giant wasn't wearing a skirt. That was his tail. He was Olokun, the one who'd dragged him a thousand miles beneath the sea. The one who he'd been sacrificed to… The betrayal of the people on the beach was withering. It overwhelmed the wonder of the merman and the palace of shells and junk. The creature (or god) must have perceived Jed's final recognition, for a slight smirk played at the corner of his (His?) lips of plum. Pupilless eyes captured Jed, a fly caught in absinthe. The eyes raked him, burned away his clothes, until his stood naked before the god. He was so weak; Olokun's presence was Kryptonite to him. Jed worried he would be soon devoured. What would it be like, to be crushed by the giant pearls of his teeth? His negritude nourishing the substance of myth. The useless bits, the gristle of Europe and the West, would be shat out, spread across the sea.

"Please," said Jed. Or he thought it. This far down, bubbles flattened and elongated. "Spare me."

Olokun, still contained by the borders of the door, shook with silent and majestic laughter. A couple of glowing fish swam on either side of his head, illuminating his face. Cowrie shells were nesting in his hair. Barnacles in psychedelic colors grasped his chin, buried in thickets of hair.

Spare you, Olokun replied in the voice of gods, *why should I spare you when you have been looking for me ever since you came here?*

"What are you talking about?"

Images, like precious jewels in a velvet-lined box, were placed in Jed's mind: the incense-soaked, shadow-shrouded cathedrals and churches he visited on the island; the self-conscious prayers to the Black Madonnas, the multiracial and androgynous Christs; the visits to the grotto of Saint Sebastian, and the fountain where he leaned languorously, in an ecstasy of arrows; the half formed prayers before he entered into bars where male beauty was of paramount importance. All clandestine prayers to remove the raised blemish on his face.

Olokun chuckled. Bubbles of power escaped from sculpted lips. *Those gods did not listen. I listen.*

Jed's heart leapt. "You—can help me?" His keloid burned.

A barely perceptible nod of the massive head. Olokun's voice boomed in Jed's skull: Why you want to remove that proud flesh from your face? You are marked. You have a map of Guinea on your face. You should be happy.

"Please," said Jed.

You must give me something.

What could he possibly give this being of lava and scales, of iridescence and shells? Could he give his soul—a kind of Faustian bargain? As Jed considered what the god might want, he was interrupted.

I will take this thing, Olokun's voice broadcast across his brain with satellite precision.

"What? Wait—"

A wave engulfed his thoughts and swallowed them in a sea of obsidian and lapis lazuli water, ground down by molars of coral, turned into particles of silt. They drifted down to the belly of the man leviathan. Images hissed away, in ghost of steam. Blond-haired Adonises, with muscles of alabaster, neither regions of coral. Blue eyes burned in the liquid furnace of Olokun's belly, as did aquiline noses and thin lips. Brown haired Jesus, tonsured men of the one God and the whores and virgins went down the ethereal intestines, to become more mulch for the bottom of the oceans. Jed was seared in flames of cold ice. He bounced in the phantom belly, and was rejected himself, of the anus of Olokun, along with the silt—

Yellow sands, and the bare feet of black people—his people— were the first things he saw. He heard the screech of seabirds, the sigh of waves, and the low singing of a chorus of people. He rolled over on his back, and found the crystal blue sky encircled by a ring of singing, concerned faces. He was back on the beach. He was sort of cold—he coughed, and seawater was expelled from his lungs, further soaking his already sodden clothes. Absurdly, the group of people began to laugh and clap. Jed thought unkind thoughts as he crashed back down into sleep.

His second awakening was gentler. Someone had stripped the clothing from his body, and placed a blanket over him. A pillow was underneath his head. But he was still on the beach. He saw the sky streaked with cirrus. He was warm and relaxed. Jed stretched, and instinctively touched the side of his face, to check his keloid. He felt nothing.

He felt again, expecting the ugly, knotted network of raised skin. He felt smooth, uninterrupted flesh, soft as silk. He rubbed again. It was wondrous, tender, but it did not tingle. Jed pulled his covering away, and cautiously stood up. He was nude, but he didn't care. The serpent sun under the sea was in his heart. He was whole again.

And the island loved him.

Circus-Boy Without a Safety Net

Lucifer came to him in drag. He was disguised as Lena Horne.

C.B. went to see *The Wiz* with his family. The movie was pretty cool, by his standards, even though he thought Diana Ross was a little too old to be playing Dorothy. But the sets were amazing—the recasting of the Emerald City as downtown Manhattan, the Wicked Witch's sweatshop, the trashcan monsters in the subway. The songs sometimes lasted a little too long, but they were offset by Michael Jackson's flashy spin-dancing. But it was the image of Lena Horne as Glinda the Good Witch that would follow him.

She appeared in the next to last scene in a silver dress. Her hair was captured in a net of stars, and she was surrounded by a constellation of babies, all wrapped in clouds, their adorable faces peering out like living chocolate kisses. He fell in love. Ms. Horne was undeniably beautiful, with her creamy, golden skin, and mellow, birdlike features. Her movements during the song "Home" were passionate. They were at odds with shimmering, ethereal-blur in which she was filmed. Indeed, she could not be of this earth. In all

of his life in Willow Creek, NC, C.B. had not seen anything like this
before.

He was in love, all right. He researched her in libraries, finding
old issues of Ebony *and* Jet; he watched old movies that she'd appeared
in, like *Cabin in the Sky*. He collected some of her records; his 8-track
of "Stormy Weather" was so worn, he had to buy another copy.

But in the weeks afterwards, he began to sense that this love of
his wasn't quite right. His brother and his father would tease him
about his "girlfriend," who was 70 years old, and about how, when he
came of an age to marry, she would be even older than that. Of how
he could never have children. His brother was particularly mean: he
imagined a wedding, held at Lena's hospital bed, with her in an iron
lung, exhaling an "I Do" as ominous as Darth Vader's last breath. But
C.B. wanted to explain that it wasn't like that at all. He couldn't quite
put it into words.

Lena wasn't an object of desire, someone who he wanted to kiss
or hold hands with. She was something more. She was a goddess
of Beauty, an ideal. She was something beyond anything he'd ever
known. She hovered above Willow Creek, an angel, looking down on
its box houses that were the color of orange sherbet, lemonade, and
his own robin's-egg-blue house. She wasn't someone to sleep with;
she was someone to be like.

C.B. made a bedroom shrine to his goddess. Old pictures of
her, protected in cellophane, marched up his wall. But the ultimate
treasure lay unseen. In the unused chest of drawers in the back of his
closet, he hid a Barbie doll, bought at a flea market and transformed
into her likeness: painted skin, eyes blackened with a pen, stolen
hair dye darkening the blond tresses. And he sprinkled lots of glitter
on her dress, so it would be silver, like hers was in *The Wiz*. (This
had involved experiments with several doll's dresses. There was a
measure of discretion; he came up with a story about how his sick
sister collected Barbie dresses, so that the store clerks wouldn't think
he was strange. He ended up dunking a powder-blue dress in Elmer's
glue, and dredging it in silver glitter. He learned it by imitating his

mother, when she made fried chicken: first the eggwash, then the seasoned flour).

But buried treasure sends out signals. Especially to mothers.

She zeroed in on the spot. Oh, there was some excuse about her wanting to check out the chest, so that she could sell it at the church bazaar. Lena was exposed. His mother and father met him at the kitchen table one day after school, holding his creation in their hands. When C.B. saw them, looking as solemn as they did when they watched reruns of King's historic speech, he knew something was wrong. He thought he was going to get a lecture on idolatry. Instead, he was told, in the calmest tones they could muster, that he was not to play with dolls ever again. That was that. His mother stood up, and started making dinner. His father left the room, his head hung in shame.

C.B. felt strange. They were treating him as if he were diseased. As if they'd discovered that he was freak of some kind. ("When your child reaches the age of twelve, his eyes will grow to the size of grapefruits…"). It was his brother that laid it out for him. He'd been listening in on the conversation.

"They think you're a faggot."

When he got to his room, the walls had been stripped. Everything of Lena was gone. The walls looked like he felt: exposed.

He didn't eat dinner that night. They didn't call him to the table.

He popped an 8-track of *The Wiz* into the player, and put the giant earmuff headphones on. Lena sang softly: "If you believe in yourself…"

C.B. snatched the tape out of the player. He unspooled the brown ribbon, until it lay in curls on the floor around him.

C.B. had a Voice. That's what everybody at the church choir said. He felt it, too. His chest would fill with warmth, the spirit of sound. And when he opened his mouth, all of that warm feeling would come sliding out, like a stream of maple syrup, rich and sweet. It would circle over the church. He could feel it soaring like an angel, over Willow Creek, notes raining down on the box houses the colors of mint-green, bubblegum pink, and pastel violet.

He convinced himself that he was singing to God. All of the ladies with their wiry hats would come up to tell him what a wonderful gift he had. For a while, he gained the pride and trust of his parents. Sort of. At least of his mother.

His father grudgingly gave him respect for his voice; but his father must've known that singing didn't really undo all of embarrassment he'd caused when he failed at various sports. Having a musician son was a poor substitute for having a normal one; but it would have to do.

Within the tiny whitewashed church, he was safe from the worst of himself. The Devil—or Lena—was imprisoned, locked away. Her smoky vocals couldn't slip in between the glorious notes of hymns. Her fabulous gowns were safely replaced by neutral choir robes.

He jumped through a hoop, pleasing the Lord. C.B. thought of God as a great ringmaster, and Heaven as a circus-dream of angels and tamed beasts. The dead could trapeze through the stars, and see the little marble that was Earth below. But first, you had prove yourself worthy. Jump through this hoop, ringed with razors. Now through this circle of fire… C.B. knew that his life would be a dazzling and dangerous tightrope performance from now on. One slip and he'd fall into a Hell of naked boys and show-tunes. The church was his safety net.

Another bonus of singing was the admiration of the congregation.

C.B. was an average student. He struggled through math and science, tolerated history and English. He didn't have any friends. Regular kids tended to avoid religious kids. Since that was his disguise, he was a loner. He avoided the actually religious kids himself—he felt that if anyone could see through his charade, they could. They would sniff it out like bloodhounds. Everyone was at a safe distance. And the holiest of music surrounded him like a shield.

He felt the most secure, when the Devil heard him sing.

He came in the form of the music and drama teacher, Mr. P. Mr. P traipsed into town in loud colors. He wore banana yellow jackets, pink shirts, and bow ties as large and comical as a clown's. In a way, he matched the colors of Willow Creek's houses. His skin was dark and smooth, like a Special Dark candy bar. He had large glasses that magnified his sad-clown brown eyes. And his hair was a mass of wild and wet Jericurls. His lisp reminded C.B of Snagglepuss, the cartoon lion. Like Snagglepuss, Mr. P was prissy and aristocratic, given to fey and archaic phrases.

Word got around school that C.B. could sing. He'd fastidiously avoided anything to do with the drama and music department. First of all, he reasoned, they played secular music. He sang for the glory of the Almighty. But the real reason was Mr. P. A whiff of his spicy cologne in the crowded school hall made him cringe; Mr. P's loud, theatrical laugh when he was a lunch hall monitor could set his teeth gnashing.

It was around January when he was approached. He left the lunchroom, walking right by Mr. P. (who wore a suit of lime-green, with an electric blue bow tie), when he was stopped.

Mr. P. spoke his name.

"Yes, sir?"

"I heard that you can sing, child. How come you haven't been around the chorus?"

"I… I guess that I've been too busy. With school. And church." He invested the last word with an emphasis he hoped wasn't lost on Mr. P.

But Mr. P flounced right by the Meaning, with a pass-me-my-smelling-salts flick of his wrists. "Nonsense. I would just love to hear you sing. Can you stop by the music room sometime this week?"

"No, sir. My course load is pretty full…"

"Any study halls?" (His sss's grated on him).

"Not this semester," C.B. lied.

"How bout after school? Just 15 minutes or so."

"Uh, this week's not too good, cause I, uh, have to help my dad with some chores."

Mr. P smiled, revealing gums as pink as deviled ham. He touched C.B. on the shoulder.

When he left the cafeteria, the nutmeg smell of the cologne tickled his nose. It wouldn't leave him all day.

That Sunday he was to sing a solo section of the hymn, "His Eye is on the Sparrow" during the distribution of the Host. Before he walked out on stage with the rest of the choir, he did a customary scan of the audience. Mr. P was there, in the pew behind his mother. His heart leapt into throat. But then, of course Mr. P would show up. The Devil can't resist stirring up souls in turmoil.

In the church basement, over fizzy punch and stale cookies, Mr. P lavished praise over C.B.'s voice, how pure it was. His mother was beaming beside him.

"Why, Mrs. Bertram—"

"Imogene, please."

"Imogene, when I heard that he had a Voice, I just had to investigate. It exceeded my wildest expectations."

C.B. kept his eyes firmly trained on the linoleum.

Snagglepuss continued: "I am casting parts for the spring musical. I'd like your son to try out."

His mother clapped her hands.

"I can't act," C. B. interrupted. He could see where this going; he had to cut it at the source.

"You don't have to act," (darling, he heard Mr. P add subliminally) "you just have to perform. And you've got that down pat." (Honeychile).

His mother pestered him into trying out for the spring musical, which was The Music Man. C.B. had enjoyed the movie, and found that he couldn't resist the temptation. It was too much. He felt Lena stirring in him. She whispered in his sleep. One night she came to him. She wore her sparkling fairy queen dress. Her chocolate star babies were grinning behind her. The only thing different about her this time was that she was in black-and-white. She'd occasionally ripple and sputter out of existence, like an image on an old television set. He took this as her blessing.

I won't give up going to church, so I'll be safe.

He landed the role of Professor Harold Hill.

The play ran four nights and a Saturday matinee. It was a success. The last performance earned him a standing ovation.

But in the back of his mind, there was always the issue of Mr. P. The jocks and class clowns of the school would always be whispering about him. They called him the Black Liberace. "Hand me the candelabra," they'd say when he passed them in the hall, or "I wish my brother George was here," in mincing voices. C.B. felt himself slipping. Movie posters of *West Side Story*, *The Fantasticks*, and *The Sound of Music* competed with the camouflage of his mother's hand-stitched prayer samplers and collected Willow Creek football bulletins.

The worst was gym class. He refused to take showers. But that didn't stop the boys from making fun of him. As they emerged glistening and nude from the showers, they would faux caress and grasp one another.

"Yeah baby, push it in harder!"

"Stab that shit, sweetie."

"Oh daddy, be my butt-pirate tonight."

He knew they were directed at him.

Summer came, and C.B. immersed himself in church activities. He became an aide for the church-sponsored camp for kids. He sang every Sunday, declining solo parts. It was a sacrifice that God might notice.

For the fall assembly, Mr. P put together a show comprised of songs from musicals. C.B. sang lead for "New York, New York," and "Send in the Clowns." He bought the house down. Basking in the light of adulation, he was mindful of the rot that hid behind and beneath Willow Creek's façade of cheerful acceptance: a hate that corroded the aluminum siding covered in pastel icing.

Church ladies in floral hats: "Mr. P, he's so, you know, theatrical. You know them theater folks."

And the antics of the locker-room boys.

Mr. P approached him for the lead in the spring play.

"I think you'd be perfect as the Cowardly Lion in *The Wiz!*"

C.B. told Mr. P he'd consider it. That night, Lena and her entourage appeared before him. And he was Icarus, tempted by her beauty. If he flew too high, she would supernova, and scorch his soul as black as the void surrounding her cherubs. He was a tightrope walker, and Lena was the spirit who watched over him, waiting to push him off, waiting for him to fall.

He could not ignore the sign that God had sent him. This was temptation.

He declined Mr. P's offer, claiming that he had to focus on his grades that semester, if he was to go to college.

C.B. did the right thing. But there was no sense of liberation.

Danger lurked, a phantom image just behind his eyes when he slept at night. He imagined Glinda turning into the Witch, snarling in frustration.

Manhattan spread out before him, glitzy, dirty, and labyrinthine. The architecture was as alien to C.B. as the Emerald City was to Dorothy. He was thrilled and terrified at the same time. There was no warmth, no open spaces like there was in Willow Creek. The buildings were naked and thin, and met the challenges of gravity head-on. The houses of Willow Creek were humble—modestly clothed in cheerful fabrics. C.B. wasn't so sure that he liked it. The crowds, the hurried pace, and the anorexic qualities of the landscape rejected him. The unending gray color oppressed him.

The Willow Creek Community College glee club had performed in a drab little church just outside of Harlem. C.B. swore he could hear rats skittering around the eaves. The nasty hotel the glee club stayed in had water stains on the ceiling, and the beds were hard and tiny. There had been a drunk sleeping in one of the chairs in the hotel lobby, his overripe smell and loud snoring filling the space. The hotel staff didn't seem to care.

Still, it had to be done. He had to test himself, to see once and for all if the Devil still lived in him. New York City was the perfect place to "experiment" without anyone knowing.

The first step was to ride the subway to Greenwich Village. He moved to the smelly hole in the ground. Its mouth was wide and yellow. He remembered the monsters in the subway in *The Wiz*. Trash cans with gnashing teeth, pillars that detached themselves from the ceiling and chased people around. What he found was a whole less interesting. The concrete floor in the subway was dirty, covered with gray lumps of long-forgotten chewing gum. He glanced down one of the platform tracks. Fearless brown and gray rats scuttled, each holding some treasure in their claws—a crust of Wonderbread, a squashed pink jellybean. C.B.'s skin crawled.

His train howled up to the platform, and the breaks squealed to a halt. He entered a drably lit car, with sour-faced people crushed next to him. He took a seat next to a blind man. The door clapped shut. His rattling trip began.

About three stops later, two men entered the subway together. Both of them wore black leather jackets, and had long beards, like ZZ Top. One man wore a tight leather cap on his head, while the other had chaps encasing his pants. When he turned away from C.B., he could see the two pockets of his ripped Levi's spread out like countries on the globe of his butt.

C.B. felt excitement wash over him. He allowed himself this one night. He had to know what he was giving up for the Lord. He stepped off the tightrope and tumbled into space.

Christopher Street was his stop. C.B. spilled out of the train and into the warm spring night. The first thing he noticed was that the Village wasn't as crowded and squashed together as downtown. There were no tall buildings. The sidewalks were thronged with people. Men, dressed like *GQ* models prowled the street. C.B. looked down. He made a decision; and looked up again. *I'm tumbling*.

He felt vertigo.

Cafes and bakeries spun past him. C.B. wandered into a bookstore. The atmosphere was thick with tension in here. Heads hunched over pornographic magazines glanced up then turned back to pictures of naked men spread-eagled and airbrushed on glossy pages. C.B. cautiously crept up to the magazine stand. He picked up a magazine, called *Carnival of Men*. He began trembling (tumbling).

The model's face was vacant. His body glistened and reflected the studio lights. His genitalia were objects: huge, flesh-colored fruits. Hairless and smooth. C.B. flipped the pages of the magazines. He found another picture, where a model spread the cheeks of his buttocks wide open. In the valley he created, he revealed the puckered rosebud of his anus.

If C.B. had been white, he would have been flushed as pink as Snagglepuss.

This is what it felt like, to give into temptation. What his mother hoped to destroy with church, what his father wanted to suppress with sports. The ground of Hell was fast approaching; it seethed with naked men and serpents. C.B. stayed in the bookstore, looking at magazines, for at least an hour. He was tempted to buy one of the magazines—this might be the only chance he got for a long time. But, then there was the chance of discovery, like his shrine to Lena. And it would be a visible souvenir of his shame.

He left the store empty-handed. The sky above the street was the sludge of sepia and purple-black, with the stars erased. There was a hint of humidity in the air.

He wandered the streets for an hour or more, putting off his eventual goal. He saw sophisticated men and women dressed in black. There were people with hair in colors of mint-green, daffodil yellow, and bubblegum pink. They wore safety pins through their ears, and some of them had white makeup on their faces, and tattoos on their arms. They were the clowns of hell. C.B. tried walking by them without gawking. He saw a shop that sold sex toys. He was too chicken to go in, so he looked through the windows, staring at the various tools and instruments of pleasure.

Finally, C.B. steeled himself. A couple of blocks from the Christopher Street stop he'd exited, there was a bar where men swarmed like bees. The name of the bar was the Big Top. He took a deep breath, stepped inside.

It was dark and crowded. Men perched on stools, sipping drinks, or clung to walls, gripping the nozzles of their beers. It was the sort of aggressive, ridiculous stance that the boys in the locker room mimicked. Others prowled the spaces between in cutoffs and T-shirts, leaving trails of perfume behind. The walls of the bar were paneled with some dark wood and wainscoted in a thick, red vinyl with large buttons on it, like the inside of a coffin.

Willow Creek was a dry county, and his mother didn't drink. His father did, but C.B. had little experience with alcohol. He went up to the bar, and asked for a rum and coke. The bartender wore an open vest. His chest was as smooth and built as those in the magazine C.B. had seen earlier. The bartender nodded sullenly, and gave him a full glass of rum, and colored it lightly with the soft drink.

C.B. looked at the drink doubtfully. He tipped the bartender, and wandered to the second room, which lay behind a black curtain.

He passed through, expecting a backroom, like he'd heard about. Darkness, smells of sweaty close bodies, groping hands. Instead, he slipped into wonder.

The room was decorated like his circus dream of Heaven. The walls were covered with paintings of elegant Harlequins and court jesters, their faces regal and dignified, not silly or sinister. One of the painted jesters wore a checkered garment of green and pink, and on the points of three-pronged hat were pansies, instead of the customary bells. There was a small stage at the end of the room. A circus dome capped the room, so you couldn't see the ceiling. A silver balloon rose from the back of each chair.

A man in a tuxedo walked to the microphone set up in the center of the stage. He waved C.B. to a table. When he'd taken a seat, the MC spoke:

"Tonight at the Big Top, we are proud to present the vocal stylings of the beautiful Lena Flügelhorn!"

The lights dimmed to spectral blue as a figure made her way to the microphone. She wore a dress of stars, her hair pinned up in some gravity-defying coiffure. A single white spotlight pierced the stage. The golden skin was a miracle of foundation. The likeness was uncanny, save for a huge Adam's apple. An invisible piano started the familiar chords to "Home."

And C.B. tumbled, plummeting to the floor of Hell. But the voice—resolutely male and tenor, yet somehow imbued with the essence of Lena—came and blew his poor body upwards, towards the star-babies of Heaven. C.B. found himself singing.

As he fell (or rose), C.B. felt Lena swell with him in. She rose up and held his hand. Lucifer—or Lena was there for him, as God had never been. If this was Hell, it couldn't be all that bad. It was beautiful here. A celestial circus of fallen stars. At once, C.B. recognized the anemic heaven he strove for, and rejected it.

Lena Flügelhorn's song ended, and with it, a chapter of C.B.'s life.

Strange Alphabets

The train was a smoking iron dragon; a mechanical monster that ate people and burped them out as greasy steam. It sat in the station huffing and farting. It was ominous, foreboding, and… exhilarating. Arthur could feel the snake of excitement uncoiling in the pit of his belly.

Adventure began in the bowels of this beast. At the end of this journey there would be Paris, with her cafes and poets. Such beautiful young men, he'd read about, with their revolution of words. No more school. No more Maman.

The thought of her, sternly garbed in black like a human vulture, made Arthur shiver, just a little. He saw her in the parlor, artlessly working at some needlepoint, her mind restless. Her sour face was frozen into its permanent scowl. Her hair, wound into its tight bun. She would prick herself with the needle. A single drop of blood, the bruised color of wine that has turned to vinegar, would squeeze forth and fall on her coarse knitting. And in that instant, she would know that he was up to no good. She was as relentless as the Old Testament

God, when it came to sniffing out sin. It was the only thing in her life. Arthur could scarcely believe that she had lain with a man at least three times. Pleasure and comfort were alien concepts to her. Her privates must be as dry and dusty as the Sahara. Perhaps her lower lips were frozen in a permanent scowl, as well.

Snickering as he rushed the behemoth, Arthur clutched the rucksack bearing his meager possessions: mostly notebooks of his poetry and a few pens and pots of ink. Clothes, he could get once he reached Paris. Harsh and metallic on the outside, the train was moist and velvety on the inside. The aisle was carpeted in crimson, like a furry tongue. The plush seats were upholstered in the same color and striped with accents of a more ruby tone. Couples sat side by side in their best. The men crisp in dark linen suits and bowler hats. The ladies accompanying them wore long gowns and sensible bonnets. Peach and lime green seemed to be favored colors. A few children were scattered here and there, in clothes that mimicked those of their parents. The girls had ribbons in their hair. The whole scene looked like an advertisement; the children were as silent as porcelain figurines.

"Excuse me!" A man brushed by him, effectively pushing him aside. Arthur realized that he was staring, and daydreaming.

Dear Madame Rimbaud,

Your son Arthur has in his possession an almost fearsome intellect. He also has an undesirable tendency for daydreaming: an effusive, allusive demeanor that effectively undermines his promise. Strict discipline will ensure that these fey tendencies will be outgrown...

Arthur straightened himself up, and marched down the corridor of tongue. The occupants of this warren politely scowled. And they had every reason to. Here was this thin, pale boy in his brother's hand-me-downs, a cross between urchin and ruffian. His hair stuck up in tufts and tendrils, a hirsute ocean frozen. His hair always did that. It would start tamed by water and the brush, but end up in disarray by day's close. The pale auburn follicles ended up in cowlicks, through chaotic hand gestures. Maman always had to chase him to cut it. The appearance of a louse would be the only reason he'd allow her scissors near. To these barristers, businessmen and their families, bathed with the lavender-scented blessings of the bourgeoisie, he was a horror. A wild creature of the underclass and the heath.

The adults glanced at him with genteel hostility. A fat girl, imprisoned in rhubarb-colored bows and a pinafore, scuttled away as he passed by her seat. In a delicious moment of impulse, he stuck his tongue out at her, the quivering rabbit-girl. She whimpered.

This car, then, was not his. He passed through two more filled with confectionary classes, until he reached a more suitable car. He wouldn't feel at home here, either. Ah, but that was Maman's voice in his head, with her aspirations. Arthur tried to find something appealing about it.

Instead of plush velvet seats, there were wooden benches, as harsh and comfortless as pews. Families sat together, in Slavic grays and blacks. A ruddy nosed drunk snored loudly on an entire bench. Even from here, Arthur could smell the sweet medicinal scent of his wine. A Jewess, her head covered in a coarse shawl, watched over her dark-eyed children. The little boy looked up at him with suspicion. As he passed them, the Jewess clasped the children to her meager bosom. A boisterous family, clothed colorfully in rags, shared a meal of stinking fish and cheese. His own stomach grumbled. He'd only had the thin morning gruel he always had.

No matter, he told himself. In Paris, he'd feast. Bakeries were on every corner, offering buttery croissants, and crusty loaves of warm bread. Cafés served dark, chocolatey coffees, sprinkled with cinnamon. Velvety soups, scented with wine and fortified with broths, tender fish, soft, piquant cheeses…

He shook himself out of the culinary hallucination, and steadfastly walked by the masticating family. They looked grotesque, like weasels given human form for a day. Towards the end of the car, there were two seats available on opposite sides of the aisle. In one, sat a villainous young man in a bowler hat and a dirty suit, long since ruined. His eyes looked shifty, and his face unshaven. To his right sat a grandmotherly woman. Her dress was dark blue and pleated. The flouncy frills of a bonnet hid her hair. A silver cross, with the tiny, tortured figure of the Savior dangled above her desiccated bosom. A Bible, well thumbed and creased, lay next to the most heavenly pastry ever.

Though the early day was grey and threatened rain, the pastry, on its napkin, was illuminated, golden, preserved underneath an egg wash. Raisins peeked from hillocks of crisped dough that swelled to suggest other treasures. Maybe marzipan, or vanilla custard. It lay enticingly against the Good Book. Its flaky sweetness rested serene on the nest of blue muslin napkin. Arthur's mouth slavered. The grandmother must have felt his eyes on her, for she stirred from her beatific repose, and smiled at him.

It was her eyes, of innocent liquid amber, that made the decision for him. For they were the eyes of the Jesus that lived above Maman's bed. Guileless circles, lit by the fire of blankness. Eyes that focused on you, with bemused blandness. Kindness that knew no darkness, but no true joy, either. Arthur knew that to eat this pastry—this, delicious, freshly baked pastry, would be to eat of His flesh. The custard would be His congealed blood. And no matter how sweet the flesh and blood, he must resist. The creature comforts were the enemies of all poets. As a poet, he must embrace the wicked and sacred at once. He turned from the offered sacrament, to the swarthy would-be criminal. A guide to Hell was what he needed now; heaven could wait.

As Arthur sat next to him, the man stirred in sullen acknowledgement. Arthur plucked up some courage.

"M'sieur, do you have a cigarette?"

His neighbor stirred, and dug around in his pockets. Slightly damp and sloppily rolled cigarettes were produced.

"Thank you, my good man."

"No problem." The man fumbled in his coat pocket for matches.

Arthur inhaled the sweet and swampy scent of the smokes after they were lit.

"I am Franz." He extended his hand, which was rough and sprouting course hairs.

"Arthur," he replied. He noticed half-moons of dirt underneath Franz's fingernails.

"Shitty day, no?"

Rain streaked the window of the clattering train. The small, irregular gems were the only things of beauty in a landscape of smudged mist and bending gray grasses. They smeared together, water necklaces destroyed by wind and velocity.

"Very shitty, yes."

The warm tobacco's fumes lessened his hunger pangs considerably. Arthur leaned back on the hard wooden bench, and closed his eyes. He was tired, after all. He fell into dream, induced by the clattering rhythm of the locomotive. Each click and clack bought him closer to the capital, with her temples and cafes, her ragamuffins and rebels. The rocking went through his body, the back of his knees, his buttocks. He became hard, and exulted in it. This journey was arousing, after all. He was a vagabond. First, he would conquer Paris with his words. Then, he would move on, to other glittering cities. Maybe London with her fogs and wretched poverty, or Amsterdam with her dens of vice and whores. Venice, with its dark canals and moss-eaten buildings, spectral cupids, and drowned saints. Or the Americas, that lawless, uncouth place of deserts, plains and religious fanatics. And from there, who knew?

Couplets, sonnets, doggerel, and sestinas—they all swirled within his head, like galaxies waiting to be born. Winged things of the finest filigree, exploding stars in violet-tinged detonations all danced within him. He was possessed! His muse was a succubus, with skin of milk and rat's tail hair. Her eyes green as the sea of the sirens. She was crowned with the secret flowers of the deep. Her feet were suppurating with wounds, blood that clotted and never fell. He longed to kiss her rank, sweet breath, and ingest the opium of art. For what were words? Mists, insubstantial, ephemeral, and female. You fucked them, waiting for the burst in the brain, the spurt of white, the rush of blood, all for ten seconds of bliss. And then you fell to the cold, unforgiving earth, and found that your wife was fat, her beauty faded. Oh, but for that one kiss.

He bent towards her, and kissed. And he found her lips hard. Whiskers brushed his face. He opened his eyes, and found the face of Izambard. His mouth was tough, his tongue questing and relentless. Art, thought Arthur, was about finding forbidden treasures, the pearl prized from the monstrous clam, the drop of blood that hardened into a ruby. If he was a criminal, what of it? The flesh was incomplete, the spirit tethered. If a muse were male, who was he to deny that? Vampire or angel, lover or enemy, all experience was the same, was to be tasted, sampled, challenged, embraced. His penis throbbed to the locomotive's tattoos, the hidden drum of the earth, the pulsing of stars. It was a private pillar that connected him to the universe. He bent forward, for another kiss—

"Tickets, please!"

Arthur jolted awake. Franz brushed him as he searched for his ticket, as did everyone in the train, including the woman with the Sacred Pastry. Arthur paused, frozen. He did not have a ticket, or money for one. He turned, and saw the clerk behind him, in his authoritarian-blue outfit. Panic fluttered in his stomach. He slithered down in the seat, a useless act, since the clerk would see him.

"Franz," he whispered. This was a gamble, but things didn't happen if you didn't risk once in a while. "Franz."

The man stopped his frantic searching long enough to stare at him.

"I… I am afraid that I don't have money for a ticket."

"What the fuck do I care?"

Arthur flinched. "You shouldn't care. Only, if you could help me, my friend in Paris shall be able to make restitution."

Franz laughed. "You little shit. You think I believe that? You think I haven't used that same line about 'a friend in Paris' a million times?"

Arthur turned away from him. He'd probably be kicked off at the next stop. And then, there would be the humiliating scene with his mother. A telegraph, and her arriving on a coach, garbed in her black carapaces like Death herself. He already felt the resounding clang as she boxed his ears, and dragged him back home like a naughty lamb. He saw the drab text of catechism; back toiling labor around the cottage. All his poems would be stillborn, wrapped in papery cauls and strangled by umbilical cords.

Something hit him, covering his face and body. He struggled with the coat that someone—Franz?—had thrown on top of him.

"Sink down, you fool," came Franz's voice through the cover of cheap linen. He felt more piled atop him. A valise or two. Arthur pulled up his legs, and got into as close as a fetal position as he could manage. He was small for his age, something for which he was thankful for once.

"Tickets, please!" He heard the collector's voice, sharp and efficient, nearby. He sensed, rather than saw, Franz handing the ticket over.

He prayed to God or any other nearby deity that the collector wouldn't notice Franz's lump of stuff breathed. I am coat and valise, wooden bench and nothing. Then, he heard the mechanical "Tickets, please!" as the collector moved on down.

Arthur relaxed. Franz muttered, "Don't move, idiot. Wait until he leaves this car."

He pretended to be wood-coat-valise until his legs ached. He dechrysalized when he felt two valises being lifted of off him. Franz was chuckling, as Arthur unfolded. His legs tingled with a thousand needles, as the blood rushed back.

"Thank you," his whispered.

Franz shrugged his acceptance.

"Why did you…?"

"I was a stupid shit, too. I still am."

He grinned back at his new friend. He would pledge fealty to him. Or better yet, immortalize Franz in words. Could Franz even read?

"If I were you, I wouldn't stay in any place too long. They'll catch you eventually, but maybe you can stay on until you get to Paris."

"Thank you, my friend."

Arthur stood in order to move to a car further down, to perhaps find a more secure hiding place. Franz stopped him.

"Sit down," he said. Arthur complied. "You don't want to move too soon. There are many tattle-tells on the train." Franz indicated a particularly nosey looking kid sitting not too far ahead.

Franz leaned forward, and whispered in his ear, "Besides, you owe me one." Arthur could smell his garlic and tobacco breath.

"But of course," Arthur said back. He shivered at the closeness of Franz. Did he feel a tongue tickling his ear? He was repulsed.

"Sit back," Franz commanded. Arthur was uncertain what to make of this change in demeanor. Franz arranged his moth-eaten coat over both their laps, and looked around the train. Arthur followed his gaze. Most people were resolutely facing forward. The neighboring Madonna had nestled down for a quick nap. This appeased Franz.

"Lay back." Franz's voice was thick and sluggish. "And close your eyes."

Arthur obeyed, even though he had an inkling of what Franz wanted. The dull mercury in the lining of his stomach stirred and gave birth to clumsy butterflies. They shone dull silver in the red-dark of his insides. His closed eyes were a screen where his could watch them bounce. He took a slow, calming breath. He was unsettled, yet curious at the mixture of dread and excitement he felt.

He heard Franz fumble with something, beneath the coat, and resettle. It was not long before Arthur felt the man's hairy paws guiding his hand to his crotch.

Franz's penis had the texture of ruined silk. Moist, dewed from sweat. Tufts of hair, foul smelling he was sure, scratched him with their composition of sweat, urine, and crusts of dried semen. In the red-dark of his closed eyes, Arthur explored this new shape. He felt the weird tree of a vein plastered on the front of penis, and followed its path with slow determination. The testicles hid in a dense forest of pubic hair. Beneath the groundcover the land was cratered and barren as the moon herself.

"Ahh." Franz let a hiss of pleasured, tobacco-scented air escape.

Arthur was abruptly bought back to the here-and-now.

"Monsieur, I cannot." Arthur's eyes opened.

Franz shushed him. "But you must."

Arthur struggled, but his digits mere twigs compared to Franz's laborer's hands.

Franz leaned forward, and whispered in Arthur ears with a sibilance that barely held back violence. "I will tell the collector of your deception. He'll throw you in jail. I've seen it done before."

"I don't believe that. In fact, you told me—"

"Hush. Do you want to get caught?"

Arthur continued in a lower tone, "You told me that should they catch me, they would send me back home. You lie, sir."

Franz paused, but he did not relinquish his grip. "That is true," he began slowly, "but you can never be sure. Policy varies from train to train. Do you really want to risk being put in chains, or having your delicate face all smashed up? A little fellow like you might even die. The choice is yours."

Arthur closed his eyes. Behind his lids, a scenario played out, of him wrapped in chains as tight as the swaddling of an Egyptian mummy, sitting in some dark, hellish cell forgotten by the Revolution, were no light ever came, and *loup garou* worse than Franz prowled, with malicious intentions of sodomy. All of his words would be burned out of him. The poet must visit Hell; he need not stay there.

He leaned back, closing his eyes in defeat. Franz relaxed his grip. Arthur resumed the blasphemous petting. In moments, the limp and wrinkled flesh (no doubt, the color of a mud besotted swine's member) stiffened. Arthur felt its fleshy length, which combined the soft wrongness of a mollusk with a center of bone, and renewed his focus on the head of the penis. In the dark, Arthur peeled back the foreskin, as if it were outer casing of some exotic fruit. The head was tender, and dribbled juices. Arthur replaced the foreskin, and peeled again. Izambard's face floated behind his lids, with eyes of kindness. He was a saint. Arthur felt Izambard's member receiving the gentle ministrations. He would do anything for that one—in palatial bedroom or dirty train. Yes—those magnificent eyes, squinting in rapture. Arthur increased the speed of his stroking. He tightened his grip on the tube of flesh, revealing then hiding the mushroom head. It felt like a thing of liquid, it was so smooth. The cock as malleable as clay, the clay of Creation.

Franz's swallowed, guttural gasp and convulsions bought Arthur back to horrible reality. A warm, thick goo dribbled down his hand. It smelled awful, worse than cat's piss. It had the feel of pulverized slugs. He removed his hand from the dying volcano of the crotch, and found his hand encased in ectoplasm. Arthur immediately began to wipe the slimy substance on the nearest available surface, Franz' coat.

"Idiot," Franz hissed, "don't ruin my coat!"

What am I supposed to do with your filth? But he didn't voice it. The slime was cooling, and left a queasy feeling in his stomach. He glanced around. His eyes fell upon the shocked countenance of saintly neighbor woman. Her lined face was frozen in a latticework of lines and disgust, her mouth a squashed O. She was no longer kindly. Her look cast him out of human society. The romance of the vagabond died, leaving behind the bitter metallic taste of criminality.

I'm sorry, mother. Her face superimposed over the woman's face for a defining moment.

The exile from the garden; the pearly gates forever closed against him. He knew at that instant that Heaven would never be his. Cain, Judas, and the struggling Jacob and his fiendish angel—these were his kin. The pagan stain of Lucifer, always on him.

The knowledge that good, studious Arthur was banished awoke something within him. It was liberating. The nausea in the pit of his stomach became the feeling of bedazzlement. It spurred him to action.

He stood up, and Franz allowed this move away from the imprisoning seat. At the last moment, Arthur snatched the coat covering Franz's crotch with a magician's flourish. Instead of a cooing dove, or a rabbit, a flaccid wormy root was revealed, to the increased horror of the kind old lady.

"You, sir, are a pervert," he announced to those who would hear. He dropped the coat in the aisle. As he prepared to flee to another car, he noticed the custard pastry, still untouched, next to lady.

"Madame, may I?" He bent toward her. She promptly swooned.

Arthur baptized the empty cloth seat next to her with the glistening excess ejaculate, and snatched the now profane pastry. He bit into the sugary crust—surely the apple of knowledge tasted no sweeter.

He dashed out onto the rickety platform between the cars. It was slippery and misty. The landscape was a blur of fields and trees, rushing by. He stepped into the next car, and was greeted by sullen and curious faces glancing up at him. Ignoring the rheumy-eyed glances, Arthur forded down the aisle of wooden benches. He took a seat next to a single woman.

Arthur wolfed down the rest of the pastry. Crisp, buttery layers crumbled on him while the vanilla-scented custard coated his throat. Each bite was heavenly. He knew that he wouldn't be eating sweets for a long time. What could he expect? A daily diet of some gristly stew, thickened with suet, accompanied by moldy bread and withered vegetables. Watered wine and yeasty beer. He ate the last bite with regret.

The woman next to him was asleep. One part of her long brown hair tickled him. Her eyes wasn't quite closed. A thin half-moon sliver of opened eye, obscured by lashes, was barely visible. Her small, high breasts rose and fell in gentle rhythm. Her skin was pale, with a thin tracery of blue veins visible at the temple. Her blouse was simple, navy blue muslin with embroidered white flowers on the V that held the stalk of her neck. The breath that brushed his face was sweet and pure. She looked like a drowned girl. An aquatic angel, pale Ophelia drifting in the lagoon, with skin as white as farmer's cheese. There was a sour smell to her, as if she had just left her morning chores before a journey to the city. What was the story there? Arthur let the gravity of sleep overtake his eyelids, telling himself that he was only resting his eyes.

Her name was Sidonie. She was going to the city to meet her betrothed; she had been sold in marriage to a creditor, to secure the farm. Her old Monsieur, who'd had a former wife and a brood of snot-nosed brats, could hardly wait to get her. Such young, unblemished flesh, waiting to be kneaded by his liver-spotted claws. Her firm, ample bosom and wide, curved hips, perfect for planting more of his wretched seed in. Sidonie would live a life of domestic drudgery, until childbirth and floor scrubbing bent her back. That is, until young Arthur came to her rescue. Oh, he was not much to look at—a waif, a bohemian poet, slight of stature, with fawn hair and a long, sorrowful nose. But he'd liberate his drowned love, and immortalize her in verse. Once freed from the clutches of old Monsieur, they would live in a basement apartment, around the corner from some squalid café. At night he would write poetry by candlelight, while she made a meager living as a haberdasher, sewing lace and ribbons on the velvet pastry of hats. Just before bed, he and Sidonie would share a glass of cheap claret wine, and, after blowing out the candles, fuck like rabbits in their junky, cluttered yet clean apartment. It was like one of Perrault's fairy stories.

Some motion, or another awakened him abruptly. He heard, "… that's him! That is the little bastard who assaulted me!"

He opened his eyes to three pairs of hostile eyes: Sidonie-who-was-not-Sidonie, her lovely face ruined with disgust; vindictive Franz, and the annoyed conductor.

"Sir," said the conductor, "I don't believe I saw you during my rounds."

Franz cut in: "He hid underneath my coat when you were checking tickets, and threatened to harm me with a knife, if I did not stay quiet."

"Did I?" said Arthur. "Where, then, is this imaginary knife of mine?" He sat up, and began to pat his clothes theatrically. "I see that it has vanished, into thin air!"

Franz sneered. "How am I to know the secret ways of criminals?"

Arthur laughed. Franz was the very model of unsavoriness, with his beady, rat's eyes and unshaven face.

"You must jest! Sir, this man assaulted me. And in a manner that the young lady sitting next me would blanche to hear. He is a pervert, as I announced to the car I had previously left. I am sure that others could vouch for me—"

The conductor was implacable; he was the apotheosis of a civil servant, brusque and stalwart. His beaky nose was the only thing that quivered on his body. "May I see your ticket?"

Arthur opened his mouth, closed it. He patted his coat, his pants. "I seem to have misplaced it. In my haste to escape the lurid attentions of—that man—I must have dropped it."

The conductor looked bored. "All passengers must have tickets." Arthur could almost see the text of the conductor's instruction manual floating in the front of him.

"But sir, surely the circumstances surrounding the loss—"

"All passengers must have tickets." This was said more forcefully. Just barely. The conductor was clearly flipping forward in his manual, to the part where the proper procedure to eject a stowaway passenger was. "Young man, please come with me."

Choice spread out before him, as long as the train aisle that he could run down. He could become some Dionysian wild man, dashing up and down the train corridors, dodging a bevy of beaked civil servants. Or he could be as crafty as gypsy, and live by his wits and discretion.

Arthur stood proud in the midst of his defeat. Sidonie looked as if she wanted to scrub his now abandoned seat with lye. Franz stood aside, while Arthur joined the conductor. Franz said, sotto voce, "Catamite."

Civilization and craftiness slipped away, like Ophelia into the dark water. The mad man took over. Arthur stood up, and pushed the conductor away, onto a hapless couple on the opposite side of the aisle.

"Villain," he said to Franz, and cuffed his ear as hard as he could. Sidonie screamed. Another woman prayed to God. Arthur snatched his rucksack, and bounded down the narrow aisle. He almost reached the door that led to another car, when he tripped. He fell, hard. No soft carpet cushioned his fall. A splintery, unfinished wood floor met his face with a hard smack. He was momentarily stunned. Then he stood up, or tried to. But something—a foot—dug into the small of his back. The toe of a work boot ground his shoulder blade muscle to pulp. Breath was expelled from his body, like juice from a grape. Arthur yelled, words, sounds. They were unheeded. He heard a mostly indistinguishable smear of babble, where he could pick out outraged and shocked voices.

The guard slid a tray in the opening at the floor of the cell. Arthur saw it was a cold haunch of some beast, rabbit or chicken, accompanied by chunk of grayish, moldy bread. His stomach stirred with hunger, or disgust. He could no longer tell the difference between the two of them. Eating the prison's food had left him ill, expelling the foul stuff from both orifices. He was not so eager to revisit the experience. The past two days he had subsisted on the metallic tasting water and eaten around the inedible parts of the bread. He crawled toward the tray. The meat was encased in an opaque membrane of yellow fat. A wave of hunger-nausea engulfed him. When it passed, he picked up the bread, which was hard and stale.

"Are you going to eat that, darling?" The rough voice of Herve, the prisoner in an adjacent cell interrupted him.

Remaining quiet, he picked up the leg bone of the portion, and slid it through the bars. Arthur continued eating his bread, softening it in the water that was also on the tray. He heard Herve's mastication, devouring the flesh.

"You are such a sweetheart," said Herve when he was finished eating. "You must tolerate this food, or you will die. Such a tragedy for such a beautiful boy."

It was all familiar now. The smells of excrement and piss, the pallet of straw, the rustling and snoring of his fellow prisoners, the dank light, the mind numbing boredom. He had been here for centuries, it seemed. He saw the cruel, indifferent faces of the guards, and the glittering lustful eyes of the criminals. From the screams and groans in the night, Arthur knew that it was only a matter of time before he was either killed, or worse. Franz's abuse of him on the train, ages ago, would seem like a tryst in a primrose path.

I am in Hell, Arthur thought for the millionth time. He moldered away in this Stygian nightmare. He lay back on the pallet, and closed his eyes, a Tantalus: outside the city teeming with poets and other iconoclasts.

Maman. How he missed her. Her sorrowful, disapproving face, her cheerless piety. Yes, even she would be a welcome alternative to this hive of depravity. One look at her boy lying in filth would crumble the blackened coal of her heart. She would embrace him; lay his head on dark bosom. A tear leaked from his eyes. He could hear her heart beating beneath the constrained clothing. The itchy hairshirt fabric, and the punishing corset of whalebones. He was just like his father, leaving her with a dingy farm.

How could you? He heard her voice, no longer soothing and maternal. May you rot, like your worthless father.

But Maman…

Her face was stone, as was her bosom. Cold emanated from her. Her heart of coal returned, her dress and corset seethed with flies: if he was Tantalus, she was a Fury, casting him into Hell with the entire world of sinners.

He cursed loudly, a sound to destroy the horrible images that plagued his mind.

"Shut up!" someone yelled.

Arthur didn't care. The hoarseness in his voice felt good. To think, days ago, he was actively seeking darkness and criminal experiences. Vagabondage held no romance anymore, not if the roads led to here. He was a fool. What was he thinking—that he would somehow escape the chaos of the war in the countryside, and live a halcyon, bohemian existence in the capital? No, Charville could be boring and stifling, but at least it was safe.

He cursed again, louder this time. The word turned into a scream, formless and piercing. It was art that lead him to this Hell. His damned, lazy, poetic nature! He was a fool. He thrashed in the straw, upsetting the droppings of rats. If he was not made of the stern, religious cloth of his mother, he was also not made of the mercurial fabric of a poet.

I curse you, Izambard, for tempting me.

I curse you, poetry, you agent of Satan, for making me see illusion and leading me into rot.

Arthur sat up. When he finally got out of here—if he ever got out of here—he swore to devote himself to his studies, learn a useful trade, and leave his childish dreams of being a poet behind him, forever. Ravenously hungry, he devoured the remaining bread, mold and all, and washed its musty taste down with the stale water.

With new resolve and strength, Arthur composed a letter in his head to his mother as he paced around the cell. He could endure her scorn for another few years.

Dear Maman, he began, *Lying here in the lice-strewn straw of this cell has made me see the wickedness of my ways. Surely, Satan has been after my soul for many years now, and only you, through your vigilance have seen him lurking around me...*

"What is this you are writing?"

Arthur jumped. The voice—where did it come from? He saw Herve in the adjacent cell, his back turned towards him; he was either sleeping or masturbating. At any rate, there was no way that he could have known what he was thinking.

"I am over here."

Arthur turned around and saw a figure sitting on his pallet, amidst the straw. He gasped. The figure was—himself. A trick of the half-light, or a hallucination? In the past week, he'd heard hardened criminals scream out in pain and madness in the pitch-black of the prison. The figure, his twin, possessed a paleness that became a ghostly beacon against the dank darkness of the prison. Though naked, he was immaculately clean, and his auburn hair stood in tufts, hillocks and peaks as sharp as knives. Something shimmered and scrolled over his body: black snakes just beneath the skin, slithering.

"You cannot cast me out," it said. The lips did not move. Phrases and questions oozed on his double's milk pale skin. Equations and formulae appeared and faded tantalizingly on the skin.

Arthur moved closer to the boy on the pallet, mesmerized. He knelt on his knees, about three feet away from him. "But I am afraid."

The flesh of this other Rimbaud was translucent, as delicate as the wing of a white moth. A tracery of blue veins could be seen underneath. And the letters of a strange alphabet, forming itself into shapes, poems and paragraphs, slid across his skin. The vowels glowed in colors, silver white, blood red, chartreuse and cerulean.

"But such visions, such adventures you will have." The other Rimbaud began to stroke his own penis, which also displayed letters. "You will live in Hell. But you will touch Heaven."

Arthur shivered. I must be going mad. But the figure sat before him. He knew that only he could see apparition. It was implicit. Maybe if I close my eyes… He closed, then opened them. The other Rimbaud still sat on the pallet, as wise and inscrutable as a statue. Arthur asked, "What is Heaven like?"

His own face smiled back at him, and there was something mischievous in the curling of his lips. "Worse than this."

A map of an unknown region splashed against that face, blue and silver, regions and shapes labeled with hair thin script.

The letter to Maman forgotten, Arthur asked of himself, "Can you teach me that language?"

A smile played on the other's lips. "The price is high."

"I will pay it." The words were so luminous. Surely it was the writing of angels. The pale him, made of words, leaned forward on the pallet. Arthur came forward, too, closing his eyes. The kiss—that transference of pressure, saliva and secret knowledge—was gentle. He drowned within himself.

"Jean Nicholas Arthur Rimbaud!" The voice came from behind him. He heard the clanking of the key in the door, the rusty squeak of hinges, and scrape of the door on the floor. "You are free to go. A friend has vouched for you, and paid your fine. Please follow me."

A guard stood in the cell door, unsmiling and official. Turning back toward the pallet, Arthur saw the illumined letters against the body of an invisible boy. They faded.

He was cursed by poetry, and it felt divine.

Magpie Sisters

Sister Magpie was the greatest thief of all, greater than the crow or the fox. Her top half was darker than the spaces between the stars. But her underside was splashed with white, where she had been burned when she mistook a fragment of a fallen star for a coin. She was a true daughter of the night. On nights of the blue moon, she could shift her shape like all of animal kind could. In her human form, she was a black woman mantled in a robe of black feathers. A single stripe of white bisected her body, from the wild tufts of her hair, down her face, through her torso. You could see the things she stole woven into a necklace: bits of glitter, a thimble, the nib of a pen. Only a glimpse, though, before the moon hid behind sapphire-lined clouds. Then she was in bird-form, off in the air, searching for brightness.

Vonda tried to ignore the calling as she walked in Greenwich Village. The vendors set things out to tempt her, wares on dirty blankets on the street. DVDs, books arranged in neat stacks, empty perfume bottles, knock-off Hermes bags. I don't need any of this shit, she reminded herself. Her room in a Queens townhouse was overflowing as it was with knickknacks. She had enough earrings to open a shop herself.

No.

She quieted the urge with the mantras Seline, her counselor, had given her. *I am strong and whole*, she thought to herself, swimming through crowds of hipsters in colorful T-shirts and gay boys in tighter versions of the same T-shirts. She had a new job (a crappy one) at a clothing store for a month; her record was going to be expunged. No way was she gonna fuck it up. But the calling was persistent. The calling was like an tickling behind the eyes, a feather-touched shiver. It quarreled in her ear, mocking and singing, just below comprehension.

I am strong and whole, strong and whole, strongandwhole. If she could just get home, call Seline.

The necklace sparkled on the ground. Vonda had never seen its like before. A variety of weird things hung between blue gem stone markers. Dice, a baby's tooth, the nib of a pen. She had to have it. The tickling behind her eyes became unbearable, as if a murder of crows were behind the mask of her face. Vonda stepped into an alley that stank of old cabbage and cat piss, to get a good look at the vendor. Even though it was relatively warm outside, as it was mid-October, the vendor was so muffled up in scarves, fingerless gloves and woolen cap that it was impossible to tell even the gender. But after a moment where the squatting vendor was illuminated by streetlight, Vonda surmised that she was an Asian woman in overalls. The rest of her wares were interesting, mish-mash hodge-podge necklaces made of wire and trash. But the blue one—Vonda could taste it, feel it in her hands, against her neck. She hadn't felt like this in months. She stopped the useless tattoo of Seline's mantra. She would steal this one, she knew it in her bones and blood. Having it would make her feel strong and whole.

The vendor walked away, not visible from the slice of sight that Vonda was granted. Perhaps there was another customer. Vonda took the chance and stepped out from the stinking alley. Into the whir of foot and street traffic. She didn't see the vendor. She did, however, see a woman standing on the blanket. Like the vendor, the woman was ridiculously overdressed. She wore a coat of napped black wool that resembled feathers. Her hat was of the same couture, except when she turned Vonda realized that it was her hair, not a knitted cap.

She was nude beneath her robe. Her hair, her body, had a single stripe of white that went right down the middle. It was a lightening strike, frozen against her dark, moist body. The black and white woman smiled. She held the beautiful necklace in her hand, offering it to Vonda.

Here. Take it.

The world was frozen, in stasis, except for the two of them. Vonda only had to make her choice and the start the world again.

When she accepted the blue necklace from the strange woman, the honks and beeps and cell phone conversations of Greenwich Village on a Saturday night started up again. Vonda stuffed the stolen treasure into her jacket pocket. She swore she heard the flutter of wings above her. Looking up, she could see nothing.

A Bird of Ice

It started with snow:

Ryuichi awoke with his feet tingling on the edge of numbness. The threadbare blanket did nothing to alleviate the chill that suffused the room. Reluctantly, he opened his eyes to the pre-dawn darkness. His roommates were all deep asleep, cocooned in their fuller blankets, yet they still shivered. Ryuichi noticed that the brazier's coals no longer glowed. With a sigh, he kicked off his blanket and sat up. He tried to spark the flint quietly, but Hideo, sleeping nearest to the brazier, groaned with annoyance. A spark jumped, bringing the coals back to life.

Ryuichi slipped into his sandals and silently padded out of the room, knowing that he would only toss and turn during the remaining hours of darkness. He went to the kitchen instead, and heated water for tea. The dark, herbal scent of the tea after it had steeped for three minutes coursed through his veins, warming him. He held the bowl between his hands, and thought of nothing. The day was a blank scroll, waiting for ink. All was sensation, and quiet (or, near quiet, as he heard the crackling of the hearth flames). Slow movement at the corner of his eye broke his trance, and he glanced out the window. Sparkling spirals of white drifted down from the darkened sky.

Ryuichi retrieved his robe and boots, and stepped out into the monastery's garden. It had been transformed. The soft, cold feathers mantled the trees, the flowerbeds, and the bridge. The dark water of the stream reflected the descent in reverse. The snow sculpted new shapes. A full moon peeked behind the clouds, illuminating the scene with silver brush strokes. The flakes kissed his cheeks, and landed in his hair. Soon, everything would be as white as a Noh mask.

Ryuichi smiled. It was moments like these where he felt the Calling. Enlightenment felt close. He remembered when his grandmother took him to the torii gate, when he was six years old. Snow had begun to fall then, too, transforming the earth.

"Stay by me," his grandmother had said. "One must always be careful when it snows. The lady of winter, Yuki-Onna, likes to snatch up little boys, and make them marry her. Then they live forever in a palace of ice, forever trying to get warm." Grandmother prayed to the kami, leaving a few coins at the feet of the fearsome statues. Then she would take him to a tea house, and slip him a bit of warm rice wine. Snow meant magic, as did his grandmother. He remembered the one time when they were walking to the gate and saw a woman disappear into a silver mist. Both of them shared the secret visitation of the winter ghost.

He couldn't really say how long he stood in that nexus of white and peace. The scene began to change with the first blush of dawn appeared on the horizon. Pink deepened into ruby slowly. He noticed that his tea was cold—that, indeed, he was cold. It would not be long before Yukio rang the bell, calling the monks to meditation. Ryuichi thought that he might as well be useful, even though he wasn't on kitchen duty today. He could bring out the rice for the morning meal from the storage shed. He started to move, when he noticed a shape in the dark pink sky. It was a large bird, painted by the light. The feathers drank the light, as if it were blood, and stained it. It flew with perfect grace, its wings a symmetry. Ryuichi gasped at its beauty.

The bird seemed to have heard him, for it changed its flight trajectory, and began to descend. Ryuichi stepped back, half in shock, and half in fear. The great creature seemed to be heading towards him. Ice and snow, feather and grace, the bird was a monstrous swan. With the precision of a jeweler, it landed on the snow-covered plum tree, and released a shower of packed snow that fell into the stream with force.

It looked as if bird had expelled an enormous packet of excrement into the water. It was such an incongruous thought, that Ryuichi started to laugh. The swan, for its part, looked offended—or at least curious—at this new sound. It craned forward the porcelain vase of its neck, and peered through masked eyes through the shifting curtain of white. This movement upset its balance. The branch was apparently slippery, for the webbed feet lost their purchase. In a cosmic cough, the ethereal bird slipped off the branch, falling into the water with splash.

Ryuichi laughed again at its clumsiness. The swan emerged from the water dripping. It spread its wings, and with a thunderous clap, attempted to take flight again. It failed in that regard; it succeeded in swirling water in the stream into froth. Impulsive, Ryuichi put his tea bowl down on the ground, walked towards the struggling swan. He stopped when he was three feet away.

The lightest dusting of frost coated the feathers, as if diamonds had been ground into them. Ryuichi looked around, for a stick or something, to help the swan. He spotted a branch that the groundskeeper had neglected on the other side of the small bridge.

"I'll be right back," he told the frantic bird.

When he came back over the bridge with the stick in hand, he saw Yukio standing outside the kitchen, holding a broom. Yukio squinted at the peculiar scene through the snow. He glanced up, and saw Ryuichi.

He called out, "You are not going to help that creature, are you?"

Ryuichi paused at the foot of the tiny bridge. "What if I am?"

Yukio chuckled. "It is just that swans are among the meanest creatures in creation. Their beautiful shape hides their nasty disposition. They are one of nature's practical jokes."

"I am just supposed it leave it there to perish?"

Yukio shrugged, What do I care? And walked away, doubtlessly heading for the bell.

Meanwhile, the bird struggled in the dark water, sending sprays of water everywhere. Ryuichi approached the swan cautiously.

He spoke in a low, and, he hoped, soothing voice: "Do not worry, I will get you out of there…"

He knelt on the ground, about two feet from the water, and was showered in coldness. He tried to ignore that, and focused on the task at hand. Inch by slow inch, he moved the stick underneath the belly of the swan, whose sodden, partially frozen wings were curled against its body. When the stick was underneath the swan, Ryuichi cantilevered the body out of its icy prison. The swan was heavy, and it took a surprising amount of effort to partly seesaw, partly pull him from the stream. A filigree of ice danced around the wingtips. Just as the morning bell began, Ryuichi removed his outer robe, and wrapped the now-stunned bird with it. Shivering, he carried his silent burden inside.

One of the younger monks was there, to start the cooking. One look at Ryuichi's strange companion caused a gasp. He jumped back skittishly.

"Don't worry, I'm just warming him up."

The monk still backed away, and left the kitchen in a flurry, probably to get the abbot, who would doubtlessly chastise him. Ryuichi ignored his anxiety, and placed the stunned swan next to the hearth fire, maintaining a firm grip on the creature. He sang a song that his mother would croon to him, whenever he had fever. Slowly, feeling and warmth came back to his bones.

The frost disappeared from the feathers of the bird, and its stunned look melted slowly. The swan made the first, cautious beginnings of movement. In the meantime, Ryuichi's feet fell asleep, due to the awkward squat-kneel he had positioned himself in. Icy needles pierced his sole and toes. In the distance, the hymns to the bodhisattva Amaratsu began, a familiar song about freeing the earth from the grip of the cold. Ryuichi thought, I would be just as uncomfortable there as here. My feet would have fallen asleep anyway.

The coddled bird began to test its mobility even more. He could feel the tension of the wing muscles, the skitter of webbed feet on the wooden floor.

"Easy there," he began.

The swan ignored him, and gave in to its animal franticness. It was like trying to hold air. Ryuichi gripped the robe that held the creature tighter. It slipped, as slippery as a whisper of silk, and the bird was free—sort of. The homespun robe was half on, half off the bird as it waddled madly about the kitchen. Ryuichi jumped up, and ignoring his painful feet, started to chase the swan. One wing broke free, and began knocking down things. A bowl of onions rolled to the floor, solid snowballs. The swan hopped-flew to the counter, upsetting dishes and cooking utensils.

Ryuichi swore. He stood still, as he watched the bird rampage through the kitchen, with attendant crashes and plops as things clattered to the floor. He laughed as eggs and ginger root and herbs fluttered in the air.

"My, but you are a clumsy thing, aren't you?" He chuckled, even as he knew that he would be severely censured by Father Iido. "Yukio was right. You're as beautiful as a cloud, and as graceless as an ox!"

The swan stopped its meanderings. A sprig of mint gently fell on its head, crowning it. It turned one eye to Ryuichi, and glared at him.

"Now, that got your attention, didn't it?"

The graceful head looked away, towards the closed kitchen door. It made a horrible noise, not unlike the sound of an untuned koto. Ryuichi jarred from the sound. "Now, you have decided to share your lovely singing voice."

A sharp jerk back of the head, with its odd and askew crown of mint. A flare from eyes as yellow as Amaratsu's golden rays.

"Listen, if you will calm down, I will open the door for you."

For some reason, he wasn't frightened that the swan appeared to understand him. His grandmother had told him and his brothers of the yosei and the fox women, as if they were real. Both his father and his mother had humored her, while giving their sons firm instruction that she was speaking nonsense. And now, he was faced with this anomaly. As monk, he was supposed to be open the workings of the supernatural world, the mysterious ways of the gods. Now, when confronted with such a wondrous manifestation, Ryuichi found it to be almost... ridiculous. Besides, he really didn't have time to ponder—there was a mess that needed to be cleaned up, and soon, before the other monks came back, expecting a breakfast.

The swan ruffled its feathers. It shrugged at the indignity of being imprisoned in his robe. Ryuichi inched forward, making the universal gestures of peace and good intention, palms gently pushing to the floor. The swan stood its ground, and Ryuichi removed his imprisoning robe from the bird. In turn, the swan puffed itself up, and spread its wings in the kitchen. It shivered like water beneath new ice, and trembled. A thousand droplets of water flew through the air, like flung crystals. They hit him, and gave his nude flesh a gentle kiss of cold. Some droplets landed in the fire, which hissed. The swan stopped when ruffling feathers when satisfactorily dry. The sun-eyes looked up at him, expectantly.

"Just a moment..."

Ryuichi ignored the eerie, alert tracking of the swan as he moved to the door. He opened it, letting in a blast of cold air. Another chant floated from across the garden. The swan regarded the door, as if it were a puzzle.

Ryuichi gestured, and stepped away from the door. "You may go, brother, er, sister swan."

The swan arranged itself for flight. The coil of yellow legs, and narrowing of yellow eyes through their mask of black. It was sudden, as gravity was ignored. Feather became liquid became air. From ice to steam, the snowy feathers a shawl, it swam through the air to the door. It was the moon shaped like a bird. It was pure in flight. Ryuichi felt it rush by him, and felt part of his soul go with it.

At the last moment, before it went outside, Ryuichi felt a tug on his face. The damned bird bit him! He ran outside, half nude, after it. But the bird had already sailed into the coral pink palace of morning clouds. Ryuichi watched as it shrank into the distance, and his face began to throb where he'd been touched.

Evening finally came, and with it, the hour that the monks had to themselves. The past week had been a grueling one for Ryuichi. While not entirely humorless, Father Iido, the abbot, was strict, and wished to keep this a sanctuary of peace and quiet reflection. Ryuichi's encounter with the swan had disrupted that ideal, and he'd been punished accordingly. So, in addition to cleaning the messy kitchen, he'd been charged with extra chores, such as cleaning the massive temple floor, making sure that the statue to Amaratsu was gleaming, and preparing the evening meal for the sixty brothers and novices. This was on top of a day of devotions, and ministering to the poor in the nearby village. By the time Ryuichi got into his pallet each night, he fell immediately into the dreamless slumber of the truly exhausted.

This evening hour, he finally had a little energy. He intended to use it, and be productive. During the previous week, he had just lightly dozed, a sort of pre-nap before the big sleep. Now, he headed to the calligrapher's studio. It was empty, save for Hideo, who was concentrating on a mountainscape. He gave the briefest of nods to Ryuichi, and went back to scrutinizing the various shades of grey. Ryuichi set up his workstation, with brushes, inks and rice paper.

He sat before the empty sheet, and saw snow and feathers. There were tiny whorls in the texture of the paper, like drifts. It was soft as down. He tentatively dipped a brush in black ink. Considered, then washed the brush. He picked one that was smaller, with a finer bristle.

A lopsided moon appeared on the page. Ryuichi resisted the urge to crumple the paper, and convinced himself that he was merely exploring creativity, rather than producing something of significance. He crossed out the moon, and began tracing the shape of a swan. But the ink wouldn't hold it. It smeared and defiled the grace. He put down his brush in frustration.

"Having trouble, brother?" Hideo was looking over his shoulder. He'd finished his painting—his workstation was clean.

Ryuichi answered by sighing.

Hideo nodded in sympathy. Though he could be annoying, Hideo had some good qualities.

"It is still there," Hideo said. "Your kiss."

"It will not go away," Ryuichi found himself saying. The right side of his cheek had a red, inflamed bump where the swan had bit him. "Nothing Haruko tried has made it go away. No poultice or tonic. I guess I will have it forever."

"It gives you character." Hideo shuffled toward the door. "I bet that you wish you had never helped that beast."

"Next time I see that bird, I'll bite it back!"

Hideo laughed. "Don't be late for evening prayers," he said before leaving Ryuichi alone with his failed painting.

Ryuichi sat staring at the meaningless smudges and smears for a good while, feeling his energy wane like the crossed out moon on the rice paper. He began to clean up the work area.

Of course, the swan, its beauty and its clumsiness, still was on his mind. Ryuichi wasn't much given to portents like some of the other monks. He tended toward practicality. But that visitation had to mean something more than coincidence. The creature had seemed to understand him!

His grandmother, had she been alive, would have told him that the swan was a yosei, that he had been marked. For a stately woman given to mystical visions, she had been surprisingly tough. She would have told him, in no uncertain terms, that he was cursed. A feeling, like the warmth that came from drinking rice wine, rose up in him whenever he thought of her.

When inspiration struck, it sounded deep and resonant, like a gong. And as the actual gong calling the monks to evening prayer sounded, Ryuichi hurriedly dipped ink in the well, and hastily scrawled on the rice paper. He'd clean up after services.

As he headed to temple, the sound of what he'd written resounded through his mind:

> *A bird of ice flies.*
> *Clouds build a heavenly palace,*
> *As the snow drifts down.*

The snow had melted. Cold, icy mud lined the path to the temple. Ryuichi was the last brother in the temple. He sat on the last mat available. Father Iido nodded, and sounded the gong starting the service. The shinshen of flower petals were strewn about the feet of the golden statue. She gleamed; there was a sparkle in to her that underscored her joy. The rays haloing her head were especially gorgeous. He'd spent all week on her; Ryuichi couldn't help feel a swell of pride in his breast.

A few songs to her were sung, of her endless kindness, and the bounty of the heavenly rice fields that graced the land. Voices rose up, like the curl of incense at Amaratsu's side.

After the songs, the abbot announced that it was time to meditate. The divine serenity of the Buddha could be felt through Amaratsu's example. Sixty heads bowed down. Fifty-nine minds went still, enfolding on themselves, reaching towards within.

One mind was restless. A thousand and one thoughts coursed through Ryuichi's brain. His mind was a babbling brook. Behind the closed lids of his eyes, he saw the floor he'd swept all week, and the mats he'd shaken out. His legs began to ache, and he worried that they had fallen asleep. His tiredness began to get the better of him. *I could meditate better if I were lying down.*

No. He must still his mind. It must be free of mindless chatter. Ryuichi tried to focus on Nothing. But Nothing eluded him, so on the screen of his mind, images appeared. Beautifully shaped kanji on fields of paper. The distant mountains wreathed in scarves of gold, mauve and lavender clouds—surely the most wonderful kimono there ever was. And, eventually, a white bird sailed amongst the embroidery. The bird in his mind landed gracefully beneath a cherry tree. Petals fell in snow showers, obscuring the bird. After the storm, the gauze cleared, and standing in the midst was a human face. There was a youth, with skin of pale gold, and hair the color of nothing. His hair, even the hair on his eyebrows and his pubes was transparent, like ice. The youth's long arms opened, beckoning him.

A scream broke the meditation. Sixty minds broke free of stillness. Ryuichi opened his eyes, jerked into reality. He heard a low rumble of chatter, as he saw the monks talking, and standing up. A group of the monks were looking in one direction: at the feet of the bodhisattva. There was a blur of movement, as something small and white dashed back and forth.

Ryuichi gasped, thinking that it was the swan, returned. But then he noticed the curl of a tail, and the nude, shriveled face surrounded by snowy fur. A monkey had gotten into the temple. The temple was near the foothills of the mountains; this was hardly the first time a stray monkey had wandered into the compound before. There was a story of a monkey that had entered the dormitory and wreaked havoc twenty years earlier, before he'd come to the monastery. The congregation watched dumbfounded as the creature galloped up and down the stage in agitated lines.

Someone giggled, when the initial shock died down. The sound disturbed the monkey, and it screeched in frustration. It hopped on the altar with its flickering candles and bowls of scented water, upsetting them with much crashing and banging.

Yukio burst from side stage, brandishing a broom. He chased the monkey around the stage and eventually into the audience. Groups of laughing and frightened monks parted like waves, to allow the figures to continue their chase. Some of the monks began exiting the temple.

The monkey darted under retreating legs and hopped on startled shoulders, the man with the broom in hot pursuit.

Ryuichi took in this scenario will dulled amusement. *See, strange things happen to everybody,* he thought. Eventually, the monkey made its way back to the stage. Yukio got in some good swipes, before the monkey scampered up the statue. Yukio cursed, and swatted at the monkey. Unfortunately, his reach was just shy of hitting the monkey. It settled comfortably on Amaratsu's crown.

Yukio began hopping like a one-legged heron, and cursing with combinations of words that would shame a nightsoil man.

Ryuichi laughed.

"What are you laughing at?" Yukio spun, and held the broom menacingly, as if he wanted to hit him. The monkey screeched, sharing his outrage.

Ryuichi got a hold of himself, and placed his hands out in a peaceful gesture. "I—"

Yukio pounced like a leopard. "You think you can do better, eh? You were so successful with that swan!"

Father Iido stepped forward, "Now, Yukio, just calm down—"

"I will not calm down! This—mooncalf is laughing at me. I am only trying to save this temple from an animal befouling it, and I am laughed at."

The abbot clapped his hands. "Yukio! Stop this at once."

Yukio sighed dramatically, dropping the broom. He stalked off the stage.

Father Iido sneered at the groundskeeper, then turned to Ryuichi. He beckoned him forward. "Brother Ryuichi, it is true that you were laughing at Yukio."

Ryuichi bowed his head, studied his slippers and the floor around them. "I am sorry for that."

"You may look up. Good. Now, I want the two of you to work together to resolve this situation."

Yukio glared at him. "Yes, Father Iido."

The abbot moved away from the stage, and cleared the lingering monks out of the temple. The monkey watched the proceedings with confusion, yellow eyes darting back and forth between speakers. As the last of the congregation shuffled outside, both men moved towards the stage together. The monkey perked up, and scuttled back towards the fan of golden rays on the statue's head. Yukio picked up his bristle-crowned weapon.

"There's another broom in the closet to the side," said Yukio. His eyes were on the monkey. The monkey tracked his movements.

Ryuichi turned, heading toward the closet. Then, he stopped. Inspiration struck him, like the poem had, as swift and sudden as lightening. "Put down your broom, Yukio," he said.

"Why? Are you crazy?"

"Let me try something."

The monkey was a living cloud of fur, floating above the ancient sun goddess. In a way, he belonged there, as one of her children.

"Go get some food. We can entice him."

Yukio gave a disgusted grunt. "Food? Why waste it on such vermin as him?"

"Yukio, please."

The groundskeeper left out of the temple, muttering under his breath. Ryuichi turned to creature, lodged like a snowball with eyes in the glorious crown.

He spoke to it, feeling vaguely silly. But then again, it had worked with the swan, hadn't it?

"Now, you don't want to stay here, do you?"

The monkey sat up, appearing to listen to him.

"I did not think so. It is quite boring. And besides, I cannot keep Yukio from you forever."

The monkey blinked in response.

"That's right. He's a sour old man. If you come down, I promise to give you something to eat."

The monkey seemed to consider it, taking on the pose of a wizened thinker, tail curled around its feet.

"At the very least, leave the statue of Amaratsu alone. Guess who will have to clean her up? The same person who has been polishing her all week!"

The monkey screeched and suddenly leapt from the crown of golden rays. Instinctively, Ryuichi opened his arms, and caught the creature. He heard a sharp intake of breath in the direction of the temple entrance.

"How in—" Yukio stopped speaking.

Ryuichi didn't answer. He carried his furry burden slowly to the temple entrance. From the periphery of his sight, he caught glimpses of the monkey's strange becalmed golden eyes. The soft fur warmed his cheek and tickled his nose. A scent of wildness wafted up, of glacial lakes, and pine trees, and the faint whiff of dung and urine. He felt a tiny heart beating against his chest. It was an eternity of careful steps. Ryuichi felt something stir in his breast. Awe? The supine figure against him exuded a trust that was absolute, almost human, as if he were carrying an infant. He felt the graceful eye of the supernatural on him. This was not normal; neither had the appearance of the swan been normal. He passed the opened-jawed Yukio, and stepped on the porch. The monkey pulled away from him a little, to survey its surroundings. He caught a glint from the golden eyes. Eyes as golden as skin in a storm of petals and snow, fur pale against indigo night, some of it dyed that color, as if it were transparent.

"You may leave now. Yukio! Do you have anything for our guest to eat?"

Yukio had become a stupid statue, holding a bowl of something in his hands. He stirred to life, like a marionette. "Put the bowl on the ground, like that. Good." Ryuichi addressed the monkey.

"Now, you may leave, but please enjoy some sweet rice before you return."

The monkey calmly jumped from his arms, and inspected the bowl. Yukio jumped back hysterically like a startled mouse. The monkey scooped some rice into its mouth, and looked to Ryuichi, as if awaiting further instruction.

"Go on, now. Go. Before Yukio comes to his senses."

A tiny paw was raised, as if in farewell. Ryuichi bent down. The monkey patted him on the face. Its paw was cool and textured, like icy leather. Then it bounded off into the night garden, over the low stonewall, heading toward the mountain.

Where he'd been touched was cool, as if he'd been kissed. The coolness spread out like ripples, starting from the point where he had been bitten by the swan.

The night was a restless one. Ryuichi felt every slat of wood beneath his body, and every thread of the blanket above him. He heard the snoring and rustling of his slumbering roommates, and the faint crackle of the brazier acutely. He could discern the fine gradients of light and dark in the room when he opened his eyes. His heart glowed with embers like a brazier. There was a delicious tension in the air, the shimmering pause before the explosive bouquet of the Emperor's fireworks display, or the displaced air after a woman's fan was snapped shut. There was no way he could sleep.

What will be next? A heron at the dinner table? A white fox at the well? He was being haunted by something. Scrutinized by something, for what purpose he couldn't tell. He, who was studious and practical, had caught the eye of something supernatural. His grandmother's tales of the yosei who shadowed mankind, performed acts of great kindness and mischief and occasional evil came to his mind. He'd been marked. What could he do to be rid of them? His grandmother was long dead; he felt regret that he hadn't really paid attention to her wisdom. She believed in the old ways, before the mainlanders bought their religion to the islands. "How is 'enlightenment' going to save us from the natural world? The sun, the earth and sea all depend on us, on our worship. We are the children of the kami."

Suddenly, when he was in the path of a sword strike, she didn't seem like such a silly woman.

Oh, he was terrified. But Ryuichi was thrilled as well. His childish sense of adventure was engaged. During his long training at the monastery, he'd never had the visions that others had. The long prayer sessions were tiring, and didn't lead him any closer to enlightenment than, say, his calligraphy and drawing sessions did.

These thoughts swam in his head, as the rafters above him blurred into fuzzy shades of blue and gray.

His grandmother had a special garden on the grounds that surrounded the house where he was bought up. She tended herbs, a few flowers, and a cherry tree. A bench sat beneath the cherry tree, which would explode with fluffy white clouds of petals for two weeks in the spring. When he was young, he loved this garden, with its beautiful flowers and its small statue to Uzume, the kami of joy. The stone goddess laughed at him as he played at his grandmother's feet. It was this inclination for dreamy idleness that marked him for the monastery, he supposed, rather than the more war-like route his elder brothers followed.

Ryuichi now sat on this bench now, beneath the cherry tree. However, there were subtle differences in the vista that made him realize that this was not exactly his grandmother's garden. For one thing, his childhood home was missing. Instead, this garden was an oasis in midst of a forest of towering black pine. The small, chuckling goddess was missing as well. Through the trees, he noticed that sky was a nude pearl color that never occurred in nature. It was like a translucent shield of rice paper, through which muted tones of lavender and blue could be perceived.

"So, I am dreaming," said Ryuichi aloud.

He felt, rather than saw the arrival of the expected guest. It was a whisper on water, or a stir of the wind, that suggested his appearance. The shimmering youth.

"So you are," the youth said in a voice like a reed flute singing words instead of notes, "and yet, you are not."

The youth was underneath the cherry tree, nearly as tall as it was. His skin was as golden as ripe pears. He was as finely muscled as any young samurai. His hair drifted in an unfelt breeze, invisible filaments, like the whiskers of carp.

When Ryuichi did not reply, the youth continued: "I met you in your world. I only thought it fair that you get see mine."

"I see."

"Are you frightened? Please, there is no reason to fear. You must have many questions."

Ryuichi could not look at him directly. It was disturbing. His face, while human, had strange aspects of the both the bird and the snow monkey—in the expressions, in its narrowness. It seemed to move, like ripples in a pond. And, the youth was nude. "Indeed, I do. I saved you the first time. Why did you come back?"

"Need you ask, my Ryuichi? When I first laid eyes on you, I fell in love. Your beauty was so bewitching that I lost my sense of balance and fell into the water. You deigned to save me, and I felt your warm hands on my body, and heard your beautiful voice. Surely, you noticed when I kissed you?"

"Is that what that was? I thought you were attacking me"

The yosei seemed not to hear that; he continued on in his callow way: "I craved your touch, I wanted to hold you, to hear your voice. So I had to return."

Ryuichi glanced at him now. His willowy limbs were too long to be really human, he decided. He moved with a sprightly grace, like an epicene noble.

"You caused quite an upset at the temple."

The youth stopped his pacing, and kneeling in front of Ryuichi, he contorted his impossibly long limbs until he was face level with him. "You are not mad with me, are you?"

Ryuichi found himself staring into gold eyes, with no whites or pupils. It was like looking into the sun.

"Not really."

The youth leapt up. He clapped his hands happily, and danced around the cherry tree. Pale blossoms drifted down onto his hair. Ryuichi noticed that he was no longer so tall; he'd adjusted his proportions.

"I was really more annoyed."

That stopped his frolicking.

"So, you are mad at me!" Ryuichi turned toward him, looking at his not-human face. There was just the slightest shifting of muscle, an undoing of flesh as it became fur or feathers. His translucent hair was both or neither. Ryuichi looked away. It was hypnotic. It made him sick.

He felt the yosei behind him. A swathe of shadow fell across his lap. But the shadow was insubstantial: a whisper in water…

Ryuichi looked up. Through his shifting face, he saw the structure of bone, and the coursing of blood.

The yosei spoke, after a silence: "I should have listened to my sister. 'It never works out, between our kind and mortals,' she warned me long ago. 'Creatures of flesh and blood that are finite and have decay built in the very bones of their being: we can only bring pain and confusion to them.' I did not listen to her; she had been a fox among foxkind for a long time. I thought her brains were addled by that experience."

When the yosei's voice trailed off, his head bowed in sadness or shame, Ryuichi felt compelled to talk. "Your sister sounds like a wise woman—er, fox. Listen," he stood, "I am honored to be—admired by you. Really, I am. But you see, not only am I human and mortal, I am also a monk, who has dedicated his life to the way of the gods and the Buddha. Liaisons of any sort are looked down upon."

When the youth looked up, his pale, blurry face was streaked with tears. Even they sparkled, like liquid diamonds. "Am I never to have you, my Ryuichi?" His flute-like voice was deeper in timbre, as if it were a flute played under water. The sight of the tear-streaked avian-simian face was too much for Ryuichi. Before he knew what he was doing, he stepped forward and brushed the glistening streaks away. They were cold to the touch, like ice. The flesh was soft, like feathers. Improbably, it began snowing. Petals fell from the tree, and he embraced the youth who wrapped him in suddenly longer limbs. It was like drowning in a sea of feathers, or petals, or snow. Sudden kisses burned the snow away, and caresses returned the chill. Wind on white wings painted by the silver moon; Ryuichi soared. The thin ether of desire burned his lungs. Then, he fell, hurtled toward the earth, crashing into a bed of luxuriant fur.

The impact was intense. He awoke, with a groan that vibrated in his eardrums. Ryuichi awoke to this: blurred rafters, threadbare blanket, cold room. This stinking flesh. No amount of kneeling and mumbling and singing could bring him closer to the divine.

Hideo was the first up: "Brother Ryuichi, what's wrong?"

"He had a nightmare about the monkey chasing him," said another monk, clearly annoyed.

Ryuichi found that he couldn't talk. He really didn't want to, either. He just wanted to be left alone. He'd been in the air, a spirit soaring above it all. And now, he was here, with obnoxious and small-minded monks, chained to the cold earth. When he didn't speak, the others gradually settled back down to sleep. Ryuichi became acutely aware that his small clothes were soaked through. They began to itch. A black wave of shame engulfed him.

"What are you looking at?"

Father Iido had crept up behind him. Ryuichi scanned the horizon from his seat on the rock, watching the clouds roll in. The sunset was truly spectacular: pagodas of orange, crimson and cream, a bold slash of color where the sun liquefied, like a rotting fruit. It meant nothing to him. He was looking at nothing; he was only waiting. What costume would his yosei wear next, during his next visit?

"Ryuichi, I asked you a question." The abbot's voice was like a bee, buzzing in his ear.

"I am sorry, I did not hear you."

Last night, Ryuichi had slipped away from his bed, which was just as well. Sleep had been impossible for the last two weeks. He had stood on the bridge one night, in the late winter chill, waiting. He heard the gurgling river beneath him. He saw the dark clouds and the fingernail moon above him. He waited for hours. *What good was a river that you could only look at?* Surely, with the *yosei*, he could swim in its dark waters, plumb its depths. And vastness of the sky, with the etched stars hidden behind the secretive clouds, its mystery would be revealed to him, only if…

A shadow had passed over the bridge, a low flying shape. Ryuichi jerked himself alert, out of his sleepy reverie. He saw silver spangled wings gliding. It was only an owl.

"…seemed distracted," Father Iido bought him back to here-and-now. His beard was white and flowing in the cool breeze. Would he ever shut up? "Others have noticed. It is like your energy has been leached away."

"I am sorry to disappoint you, Father."

Any moment now, he would come. A monkey or a swan. And Ryuichi would follow him. And he would be away, in the heavens, or beneath the sea. All of that would not matter, if he could be with the *yosei*, wrapped in his willow-long arms.

Father Iido slapped him in the face. It stung him. Ryuichi was no fighter; but as his father's son, he'd received slight training. Instinctively, he leapt to his feet, and made to attack the aggressor.

Iido laughed: "Finally, some life in you."

Ryuichi relaxed out of the position. Yet another distraction, yet another speaking, decaying sack of meat.

"What is wrong, son? You used to be one of the most impulsive people I knew. Are you homesick? Are you rethinking your initiation to the order? Speak to me!"

Why couldn't the old man be quiet, and leave him to his waiting?

Ryuichi lied, "I am feeling a little ill, these days."

Father Iido clicked his tongue against his teeth. "No doubt, because you've been wandering around at night. Do not think that I don't know about that."

Ryuichi looked at Iido's face. He was as withered as a dried fruit, with skin of leather. Humans were such vulnerable things. "I…" he began. But no words could explain how he felt. And it was shameful, to say it. *Remember that monkey that got into the temple? Well, he is really a creature of myth that has fallen in love with me. And I love him, too. I am just waiting for his return, to let him know how I feel. You see, he let me feel his world. And it is nothing like ours. Colors are sharper. Music flows through everything. You can hear the stars laugh, and smell fragrances that you never thought possible.*

Father Iido considered Ryuichi's silence. "You are ill. But it is with soul sickness. I have been here for over forty years; I know that look. There is only one cure." Ryuichi waited patiently for the old man to finish: "Prayer. Meditation."

Ryuichi bowed, nodding his head.

That evening, the monks filed into the temple like silent puppets. Ryuichi sat on his knees, and closed his eyes after the last gong resounded. More waiting. Maybe he would see the youth there, behind his eyelids. It was as good a place as any. An acolyte began a low humming chant.

Ryuichi waited for a sign. His entire body felt tense with anxiety. Every coiled muscle in his neck and thighs waited for release. Through a profane act, he'd been allowed to see eternity, to taste it. The sacred no longer held any allure for him. Surely, the spirit could hear his psychic cries for help, feel the wave of desire for union.

It began with a tingling in the pit of his stomach. A presence heard him, and Ryuichi left his body behind. The room and the chanting all faded into the background. He was enveloped in cloud, caressed by it. He waited for the mist to clear, to see the weird, elongated face of the swan boy. His heart swam in anticipation of seeing the face, and his grandmother's garden.

Cloud refined, reformed, and reshaped itself. Wispy, translucent trees grew in the distance—a ghostly pine forest. A monstrous willow tree draped shredded white leaves over a lake of sapphire. He found himself surrounded by the lake, in a small island of cloud, with flowers sculpted of water, and lace bonsai trees. This sanctuary was beautiful, the perfect place to meet his strange lover.

Ryuichi stepped to the edge of the impossibly blue lake, and found that it wasn't a lake at all. It was the sky. Birds flew below him, and further below were the pitiful bottom dwellers—humanity. He'd left it behind, including his body, for a grander existence.

He turned around to survey the garden of cloud, and found that he was not alone.

She sat on an ornately carved throne, decorated with serpents of blue and green. If you looked closely, you could see them moving, slowly. Her red kimono moved with the molten grace of lava. Her hair was blue-black, and framed her bright, golden face. He found that he couldn't look at her very long. It was like looking at the sun.

With a gasp, he knew who it was. Ryuichi hastily fell to the (white) ground, and bowed his head.

"Stand up, young man." Her voice was imperious, but not without a sparkle of humor. "You will find that flattery gets you everywhere; however, it does get tiresome."

When he stood up, Ryuichi found that the throne and the lava dress were gone. In their place was an old woman, with hair as white as cloud, wearing a simple robe of blue. She stood next to a wheelbarrow full of cumulus flowers with cirrus petals. In a distant corner of the sky, there was a glitter of movement: the serpents spun through the air like acrobatic eels.

"Divine Mother," he began.

She held up her hand, stopping him. "Enough flowery talk. You may ask any question you wish, but please, no more 'divine mother.'" She promptly bent down, and pulled another flower from the ground.

Ryuichi walked next to her, apprehensively. "Divine—Please excuse me, but I can hardly call you, 'You, there.'"

She laughed, putting the flower into the wheelbarrow. "I always did like you, Ryuichi. You have a wonderful sense of humor. Or at least you did, before that creature had his way with you."

A cloud bubbled up behind her, and she sat down. She gestured for him to do the same. Ryuichi found that a similar 'seat' had appeared behind him. He sat down. It was as soft as feathers.

"So I am cursed by the *yosei*," he said with a sighing.

She rolled her eyes. She was nothing like her image, which he had obsessively cared for over the past month. And yet, her divinity surrounded her.

"What is a curse?" she said. "Men curse themselves; they need no help. That particular *yosei* loves making mischief; he has a peculiar fetish for chastity and piety. Imagine the nerve of him, sitting on my head with his dirty behind!"

"You know him?"

"Who don't I know? Listen, let me let you in on a little secret."

Ryuichi leaned in close.

The Divine Mother whispered: "It's all the same. Demon and god. Earth and air. Snow and petal. Swan and monkey. The sacred and the profane. It's all a matter of perspective."

Ryuichi sat back. "I don't understand what you mean."

The bodhisattva leaned back, as if she were considering something. "Years ago, when I was much younger, and more foolish and self-centered, I had a bit of a conflict with my brother. He can be bit, how shall I say, insufferable at times. He was flexing his muscle, exulting in his power, much in the way that warlords on earth do. You know the type, eh?"

Ryuichi nodded.

"So I went into hiding. I was as sulky and ill-tempered as that little groundskeeper man Yukio is. You see, I was a bit, how should I say, vain. As a result, the world and the heavens were plunged into darkness, for many years. But I did not care about anything but my own rage and annoyance at my brother. Ah! And no-one could lure me out of my hiding place. No one, that is, except Uzume. How I love her, my whirling sister!"

Ryuichi remembered the laughing stone woman in his grandmother's garden. She seemed to be the *kami* his grandmother liked the most.

"It all came together, through her nasty, lewd dances. Shaking her breasts at me, showing me her nether regions, she reached me where prayer could not." She paused, as if waiting for a response from him. "You see, carnality and the pleasures of the flesh—laughter—are not antithetical to divinity."

Ryuichi nodded, stupidly. He said, "To be honest, Divine Mother, I still do not understand."

She leaned forward, and gently patted his hand. He felt her nascent heat. "Do not worry, child," she said, "You will."

She stood, and kissed him gently on the cheek, on the spot where he had been marked by the *yosei*. Ryuichi expected to be singed. And he was, but not on his cheek.

The heavenly isle melted, and he felt himself spiraling downward, toward reality. He caught a solar flare glimpse of Amaratsu, in her divine form. It burned his eyes as he fell, through clouds as soft as fur, and petals as cold as snow.

Spring arrived two weeks later. Buds appeared on the trees, and the ground sprouted young grass, green stubble on the black skin of the soil. Cautious birds appeared on the branches, and flowers rose from the earth. The days lasted longer, and all was drenched in the perfume of growth.

Like the world around him, Ryuichi was revitalized. A new energy coursed through him, no doubt granted by the *kami*. He filled the hours with activity. Mornings he would help the surly Yukio with his yard work. After a while, the groundskeeper began to grudgingly accept his presence. He taught village boys writing, and nights would be spent working at his beloved calligraphy. Meditation and prayer came easily to him; the possibility of another visitation was always there. Iido was pleased, and pulled him aside after a service.

"You seem to have rededicated yourself to your life here. You are no longer soul-dead."

Ryuichi smiled, and gave a slight bow. "I wish to thank you for your advice."

Iido nodded brusquely, and never bought up the subject again.

The secret light of the *kami* shone in everything. Every drop of water was a prism that reflected her in rainbow colors. The warmth of the air, the raw glory of sunset—all were reflections of the Way. For the first time in a long time, Ryuichi felt that he truly belonged here. He was not merely the dreamy younger son, left here for lack of fortune.

Ryuichi walked to his room, full of joy. It had been a wonderfully full day. There had been a visit to the village, to share food with the poor and infirm, followed by an intense walking meditation led by one of the acolytes, around the foothills of the mountain. The families had been grateful, and he recalled that as he heard birds singing brightly. Ryuichi remembered his grandmother, the walks that they would take together, down forest paths and by the sea walls. The warmth of rice wine in his belly, the taste of spring on his lips. Her stately gait, his hand in hers, held tight.

Ryuichi was flushed, and glowing, when he entered the room he shared with the other monks, looking forward to a long and restful sleep. He entered the darkened room. Past the threshold, he was hit with chill air. Early spring nights were chilly, but it was colder inside than out. The brazier was not lighted, which was odd. He stood for a few moments adjusting to the dark. Black became grey, and lumps became human bodies, huddled underneath covers. Arms and legs, rising chests. He moved through twilight, to his own pallet, and saw the multiplicity of limbs and legs spilling from the others' beds. The silver hoarfrost of sleeping breath mingled about supine forms. Two to a bed, entwined against each other for warmth. *Why don't they just light the brazier?* And movement, the melding of bodies beneath the grey covers, the anguish-wracked faces. Ryuichi gasped. But of course, not everyone could resist temptation. It was a struggle, eternal, the sundering of body and spirit. Still, it was shocking, to see male lovemaking right in front of him. Ryuichi removed his clothes and sandals in the dark, and dressed in his sleeping clothes, steadfastly ignoring the pulsing forms in the pallet near him. He heard groans, and closed his eyes against them. Limb on limb, the curve of bodies, the hollows, the masculine scents, all blending in his vision, his ears, his nostrils. Ryuichi shivered.

"Are you cold?" Hideo's voice was at his ear. Ryuichi opened his eyes, and saw Hideo standing next to him, wisps of fog falling from his lips and nose.

"Yes," he whispered. "We can light the brazier."

Hideo nodded. "We could. Or, we could do this."

Hideo leaned close, and kissed him on the lips. He held Ryuichi's shoulders, and lightly kneaded them. Ryuichi kissed him back, and explored the cave of his mouth with his tongue. It was cold. The teeth he lightly licked where icicles. He pulled back.

Hideo's face was *wrong*: the expression was slack and malleable, as white as clay, and sugared with frost. Ryuichi moved back, away from Hideo. He now stood still as a statue. All color had been bled from him. His skin was white. The color of—

Ryuichi looked around the room. Figures still writhed underneath covers. Frost glittered here and there, like crystals. Ryuichi stepped back. He saw the cold brazier, the wooden slats of the floor, the moonlit window. He discerned every shadow in every corner.

"Show yourself," Ryuichi said. His voice shook; he was chattering with cold. He repeated himself, a little more firmly this time: "Show yourself!"

In the dark left hand corner of the room, the air coalesced and thickened. Squinting his eyes slightly, Ryuichi could make out a form there. A suggestion of wings, the stem of a neck. Etched on the darkness, a transparent bird. It was a bird of ice. The topaz beads of its eyes glowed faintly in that dark corner.

Ryuichi jumped—he felt Hideo's hands on his shoulder. Cold fingers dug into his shoulders. He felt Hideo press into him, fit the contours of his body to Ryuichi's. Ryuichi felt the pull of his answering lust.

It was hollow, and cold. The bird of ice watched the two monks, swaddled in the dark clouds. Ryuichi echoed inside. Hideo, or the *yosei*, unfastened his robe, and so, unfastened his soul. It was like a soft falling away. Of petals from a tree, of white feathers from a leaden sky. Of a woman vanishing into silver mist.

That day with his grandmother, coming from the *torii* gate, came back to him. They'd stood together for long moments, after watching her fade away.

After a while, his grandmother spoke. Her voice crackled with age and wisdom, like the beads of a merchant's abacus. "A ghost is a soul that is not connected to Nature. They have fallen off the path of *kami*. It is always very sad."

Five-year old Ryuichi had looked up at her. He saw her hair, as white as the snow that fell around them, the wrinkles on her pale face. *Surely, no-one is more connected to Nature than my grandmother.* She broke the somber mood by taking his hand and taking him into the teashop, and gave him a taste of sake, that burned his fear away. "Now, don't you tell your mother about this!" she'd said, merriment in her eyes.

The glow of the sake, the leathery feel of her hand, he felt them now, even as the *yosei* stared on, as Hideo tried to arouse him. That glow spread throughout his body. It went from his belly, up his spinal cord, through his arms, up to his brain. It rested in his eyes. Ryuichi felt that he had drunk down the sun. He was warm, with the love of his grandmother, the wisdom of Amaratsu, and his connection to the path. Surely, he glowed. He gave into it all—the ghost bird, the haunted monk, the caresses. It all had a place. Ryuichi smiled. The smile was a ripple, a current of warmth that reverberated across the room like an earthquake. The bird in the corner faded, melted into shadow. The topaz eyes dulled, and Hideo's hands fell away from his body. Ryuichi watched as he trance-walked back to his own bed. His two other roommates separated, and sleepwalked back to their own pallets.

Ryuichi was left alone in darkness, as he watched the sleeping monks. It was dark, but he still glowed inside.

A low gong signaled the end of the ceremony, and Ryuichi opened his eyes. He stood, and stretched, feeling oddly refreshed. As he headed out of the temple and into the night, Hideo stopped him at the door:

"Brother Ryuichi, the stain on your face is gone," he said.

He touched his cheek. It was still warm.

Ryuichi smiled. "You are kind to notice, Brother Hideo."

Catch Him by the Toe

He appears on the evenings of summer nights, when the humidity reaches the point where it can no longer be tolerated, when even the flies hide under leaves and even breathing unleashes a torrent of sweat. He has been seen on the lawns of Wisteria Heights, the streets of Darktown, or the alleys of Clovertown, all over the sleepy town of Azalea. At first, the witnesses were not credible: children with overactive imaginations, town drunks, ladies out when no decent lady should be about.

The giant is always shirtless, his torso rippling with muscles. His skin is darker than night, and striped with starshine lines. His bald head is an ugly shade of purple, the color of wounds and organs hidden deep within the body. The face is savagely handsome, save for the bulging, veined eyes and the burnt, blackened tongue that sticks out; it looks like the mask of an Oriental demon. His hands are tipped with diamond-sharp claws. But the worst thing about him is his eyes. They are a soulless, relentless green, with the slits of a cat's eye in their center. He is haloed by red-gold flames that burn tiger-bright before the image snuffs out.

The Azaleans, the old timers, never speak of the horrible apparition, and newcomers quickly learn to keep quiet about it. Most folks stay in their houses, and close their shutters, in spite of the creeping heat. They know they're his prey.

Eeny, meenie, miny, moe...

Azalea was under glass when the circus came to town one August night.

The air was close and still. The darkness teased; it looked like a cool shadow, but oh, the treachery! Houses sweated. Fans swirled dead air. Cats and dogs hid under porches, with the roaches. Piles of manure smoked, even though no sun was present; who knew that moonlight could be just as unforgiving? No amount of iced tea, lemonade or hooch could relieve the restlessness. The heat hugged you, like an aunt whose affection you had to endure.

A child first noticed the caravan of lights piercing the muggy, dark air. That child, or possibly a sibling, spread the word. Gossip was like locusts in Azalea: quick and relentless. Because nothing ever happened in Azalea.

Pretty soon, a collection of folks gathered around the campsite, both colored and white, to watch the exotic circus folk set up their town. They started at once, industrious as elves. Clang, bang, whir. Their activity stirred up dust devils. Not that the town folk minded the sounds. Sleep was a distant memory, a myth. Watching the fantastic city being constructed in front of them was the closest thing to a dream they'd get tonight. Everyone in the impromptu crowd grew silent as they watched lumber transform into booths and lumps of fabric become tents.

Townfolk tried to catch glimpse of the star denizens of the enterprise. Was that young, swan-like sylph sipping Grape Nehi an aerialist? That hooded figure, sulking in the doorway, taking a smoke break, surely he was one of the freaks. People claimed they saw a bearded lady, a contortionist, or a wolf-boy. Whoever the circus folk were, they wasn't friendly. They flitted by, not granting the crowd a single glance. A swarthy group of men—Italians or Mexicans, it was hard to tell in the dark—unrolled a fence, right in front of the crowd, effectively blocking the view. That broke the crowd, and back down the dusty roads to their hot little houses they went.

A scream split the air. The Azaleans stopped in their tracks, a sudden chill crawling down their backs. They turned, and heard the awful screech again. Even the damned cicadas paused. The scream wasn't human. It was fierce, yellow rage, striped with black hate. A low murmur broke out amongst the folk, one of excitement mingled with dread.

The next day dawned yellow and red, like a bloodied yolk. The mercury in the thermometers held its stubborn place. It was too hot to visit the dustbowl site of the circus. Most everyone kept inside. Rumors surfaced here and there. At the General Store, one of the Azalea society doyennes swore that she saw a midget man and his lady down by Magnolia Creek, daintily stepping over the bridge, both in child-sized adult clothing.

A group of colored children, peeking between the slats of the fence, claimed that there were alligators, elephants, monkeys and a couple of vampires.

The pious prayed for the populace's souls, in churches and revival members' living rooms.

As the heat of the day ebbed, a group of curiously garbed men marched down Main Street with flyers and posters. They wore ruffled, white pirate shirts, loose purple britches sashed with a black strip of fabric, and shiny black boots. There were seven of them. Two went downtown, two uptown, and two went into the poor section, with its Irish and Negro populations. One stayed on Main Street. He didn't carry any posters or buckets of glue. He wore a sandwich board, plastered with two posters, front and back. The front poster showed a nimble ingénue, in pink tights and a spangled skirt. She pirouetted on a thin wire above the gasping crowd. A plume of flamingo-pink rose from her quartz tiara, and formed one I in the sign proclaiming her Ariella, The Flamingo Girl. Below the picture came the announcement: See the princess of the high wire, as she dances in a death-defying ballet, where Balance is Supreme, and Gravity is a Nemesis!

The back poster featured a shirtless blue-black African brute, his muscles straining, and sweat pouring down their architecture in glimmering rivers. His flared pants were shocking white against his dark skin. With his bare hands, he held two snarling tigers at bay; his thick, superhuman hands throttled their gold and black necks. One tiger raked his chest. Bright blood showed in the gashes. And, yet from the picture, you did not know who was more savage. The bestial look on the black man's face rivaled the open-mouthed wildness of the tigers. In a half moon about the scene, were the words, See Sambo and His Tigers! Underneath, in the red letters of boys' adventure novels: From the Heart of Darkest Africa, comes a Master of the Beast. This Sambo turns Ferocious, Man-Eating Tigers into Kittens!

The two in the hoity-toity section of Wisteria Heights were successful, if only because their pasted lurid posters incurred the immediate wrath of the residents. A procession of grande dames and their hapless husbands descended on the carnies, explaining that they had to go through Mayor's office to get permits to hang signs. Not that it would matter; Wisteria Heights, with its ivy-clad manses, was a historical area, governed by abstruse standards and protocols. The carnies assiduously ignored them.

The unofficially named Clovertown welcomed the carnies with open arms. Cold beer, soda bread and cigarettes were offered to the men, as they affixed the posters to poles and the sides of businesses with as much sweat as paste. There was something magical about their appearance. It was a break in the monotony of life.

The Negro section of town thought that the carnival signaled a different, sinister kind of magic. The men assigned to poster Darktown were as silent as ghosts. They seemed to be unaware of the gathering group of children following them. It was eerie;

a debate sparked amongst the children as to whether or not they were phantoms. Against pool hall and liquor store, gleaming Sambo wrestled his tawny enemies. The nightmarish images inspired mamas, aunts and sundry ladies to disperse the groups of kids and corral them back to home and their chores. The Baptist minister was alerted. He emerged from his home and made a half-hearted attempt at fire-and-brimstone assaults. There was something devilish about the pictures of midgets, nymphets and half-nekkid men. It was wicked entertainment, leading spiritual decay, pleasures of the flesh, lack of ambition, etc. But the heat—and the unresponsiveness of his targets—got to him.

Soon, the entirety of Azalea was postered and leafleted. You'd have to be blind or senile not to know about Fiorelli's Carnival. By the time Friday rolled around, a line of Azaleans and members of the surrounding towns was waiting at the causeway. Not a few of the folks in the line were denizens of snooty Wisteria Heights—there presumably to mingle with the hoi polloi and report on the invasive crassness.

Once past the ticket gate, a customer was transported into a shimmering citadel of peppermint-colored tents, creaking rides, and dusty lanes, all held together by the luminous web of electricity and neon. Smells assaulted the nose: the buttery sizzle of burnt popcorn, the oil and gasoline reek of the rides, the stench of the unseen animals. No person emerged from the makeshift town unmarked, with dust and the lingering miasma of the perfume of too many bodies crushed against one another. All told, most found that Fiorelli's Carnival deficient.

For one thing, the sideshow attractions left much to be desired. The Bearded Lady, for instance, simply looked like a man with a dress on. Several people swore they saw the "lady" scratch her balls when no one was looking. A number of the same group claimed to have seen him go for a piss—during which she stood, after hiking up her skirts, and let rip an arcing yellow stream. Upon seeing the mannish, slovenly woman, it was easy to believe.

The midget couple, advertised as Mr. and Mrs. Tiny, were downright rude. When curious children attempted to touch the doll-like Mrs. Tiny, she told the kids to "mind their manners." One affronted mother expressed her displeasure; to which the pint-sized lady replied, "Keep your grubby children's paws off me; these frocks were made in Paris—not that a hick like yourself would know the difference." Certain members of the population found these kinds of antics to be highly amusing. Kids and adults loved to heckle the pristinely dressed Mrs. Tiny, working her up into a frothy rage. Beribboned and pearled in confections of crinoline, lace and taffeta, she resembled a rabid poodle when her ire was raised. Mr. Tiny, for his part, would act like the classic henpecked husband, attempting to soothe his spitfire wife. Embarrassment was writ large on his diminutive face.

The fat man—who, at 500 lbs was 45 lbs lighter than another Azalean—looked supreme in his boredom. The fire-eater burned himself severely, and was out of commission by Saturday.

The only redeeming feature of Mr. Fiorelli's debacle was the big top show, which began with an explosion of confetti from one of the cannons—out of which a clown tumbled acrobatically. The flat-footed entertainer was immediately joined by a clown troupe of graceful harlequins to bewhiskered hobo types. They scattered around the bleachers, finding targets in children and willing adults. Mock fights would break out on the floor, with flying pies and seltzer water bottles. Meanwhile, flowers and eggs would emerge from audience members' ears and underneath hats. Some clowns were a bit more ribald. One sneezed quarters; another one pretended to have problems with gas. An unlucky victim would be showered with flower petals after a honking noise was made. A sharp, military whistle stopped the assault on the audience. The clowns assembled in an orderly line. Two more shrieks of the whistle, and the clown from the left knelt down as the clown to his right climbed atop his shoulders. Much hilarity ensued when a short clown struggled to balance on his gigantic brethren. Further whistles caused even more outlandish formations, with mishaps. The final formation was a requisite pyramid, which, to the squealing delight of the children, collapsed quite spectacularly.

Darkness fell like a curtain. A single spotlight pierced the dark, revealing an elegantly attired man in a top hat, tuxedo and tails. "Ladies and gentleman," he intoned through his red megaphone, "no introduction is needed for Ariella, our glorious flamingo-girl. You will have heard, no doubt, that we found her as a babe, in one of the tropical isles of the Caribbean. Someone had left such a precious babe in a nest; she was raised by a flamingo, and her brothers and sisters taught her secret of balancing, if not of flight. I, Fiorelli, rescued her from her avian youth, taught her language and manners. But she still retains memory of life among the flamingoes. Behold!"

(This spiel was listened to with uncomfortable patience during most nights; both nights reserved for colored audiences, someone would interrupt the solemn Mr. Fiorelli. One night, a person yelled out, "Did she hatch from an egg?" which elicited howls of laughter).

The spotlight on the floor would fade which would be replaced by a blue beam, trained on the high wire. Ariella, garbed like a ballerina, would be in flamingo stance: resting on one leg, the other folded up neat as an umbrella underneath her skirt. An amplified Victrola would start up with some piano arpeggios, blue became white lights and Ariella would unfold like a hot pink flower. She ran the length of the wire the size of a thread. The rest of her routine had her doing similarly death-defying feats, dancing on the razor's edge of clumsiness. She'd skip, walk on tippy-toes, and tumble, all without breaking a sweat. It was surmised that there must be some harness underneath her vestments. At the performance's end, she leapt off her roost, and plunged into a safety net, in an explosion of magenta plumage. Wild applause thundered beneath her. After a brief mime-show interlude, the Flamingo Girl would reprise her role, this time as a mistress of the trapeze. A troupe of surly Russians flung her through the air like an exotic scarf. Her porcelain face was frozen in a permanent grin as she sailed above the populace of Azalea. They felt kinship with her, even if she was a bit of a fraud. After all, she was dressed in the same color as the town's namesake flower. (Not all Azaleans were so generous, though. One of the hecklers from the colored nights remarked that she was unaware of "a whole lotta Slavic-lookin' folks in the Caribbean," that it was news to her.)

After this portion of the show ended, all lights extinguished. The lone beam burned down on Mr. Fiorelli. The Victrola played a low tattoo of drumbeats, as the ringmaster began his recitation.

"The Dark Continent is a place of unparalleled savagery and ferocity. It is a land of mystery and splendor, full of dangers, strange people, and truly fearsome creatures. The gigantic giraffe, the monstrous rhinoceros. Snakes the size of trees, and the noble lion. None of these beasts is as terrible as the man-eating tiger!" Out in the darkness, a whip cracked. In response, a hot-yellow roar emerged from somewhere. The folks in the front row jumped. "I heard of a tamer of tigers, deep in the wilds, during one of my visits to Africa's shores. I simply had to see this for myself. So I went into the heart of the jungle, on a quest to see this legendary man.

"It took many days, through perils you can only imagine. Past pits of quicksand, and caves of vampire bats, and nests of vipers. Past the land of the mighty gorilla!" (Fiorelli paused every now and then, expecting gasps of awe. Sometimes, he was obliged). "Finally, I reached a small village of savages in the middle of the jungle, men with bones in their hair, their ladies as naked as the day they were born. This tribe had a special meal they liked to prepare—a real delicacy. During certain times of the year, they would eat human flesh!

"As you can imagine, I was more than a little nervous. I am sure that they had never had Italian—ha ha! Anyway, this tribe regards tigers as sacred. And they had a young gentleman, who you are about to meet, who was friend and lord of the sharp-clawed fiends. (A heckler pointed out, "Tigers don't live in Africa!").

"Needless to say, I was quite impressed. I convinced Sambo here—his real name is some unpronounceable African one—to join us. Ladies and gentleman—prepare to be amazed!"

The drum tattoo reached a crescendo before suddenly stopping. The spotlight trained on Fiorelli turned off. Slow as a veldt sunrise, lights revealed a cage in the center of the floor, filled with two large black and gold tigers, and one that was pale as a ghost, even as he was striped like the rest of them. The beasts rested raised on cushions. In their midst, as imposing as the creatures themselves, prowled a gigantic black man.

But "black" did not describe him. Basalt, onyx, or sable—these words did him more justice. His skin was smooth as satin, and glowed with a purple luster. It was bright black, if such a thing could be said to exist. As depicted in the posters, he was shirtless. His chest glistened in the hot spotlights, even reflected them. He wore purple pantaloons that ended just about his shins; the ruched legs were ringed in silver. Sambo's face was harsh angles and planes, his eyes were wide and almond-shaped, his nose flat, the nostrils flared. He was the embodiment of all that was known—and unknown—about the Dark Continent.

The audiences gasped and held in their collective breaths. Just as air was about to be drawn into deprived lungs, the giant—for he was at least 6 foot 7 if an inch—stopped his restless prowling. He faced his captives, fixing them with an unswerving stare. He shouted a single word, in an alien tongue. His three wards raised themselves in this order: orange, white, orange. On their cushions they stood, stretched, and emitted hot, cindery growls.

The sides of chairs were gripped.

Without a moment's pause, Sambo clapped his hands, and the beasts leapt from their perches, landing on the circus floor with thuds that people in the bleachers felt. They circled him, with snarling faces. Sambo stood in their midst, statuesque, oblivious. It was like a grotesque merry-go-round, graceful monsters encircling a living sculpture.

Another shout halted this activity. They bowed, the tigers, their heads down, a paw extended out. At another word, the tigers withdrew their paws and raised themselves on their hind legs. They proceeded to spin around in lazy circles. Sambo placed his arm around the "waist" of the upright white tiger, which rested one paw on his shoulder. They danced a minuet for a minute. This silly spectacle relaxed the crowd; hands tentatively let go of each other and chair sides. Giggles, titters and laughs escaped.

At that point, Sambo uttered a word. The tigers dropped to their fours, and growled again. Soda pop sloshed, popcorn buckets jumped at this sudden change of behavior. At another command, they stood on their front paws, and held absurd poses for a moment before dropping on fours again. Sambo snapped his fingers, and the tigers scattered to three corners of the cage, and flashed their razor-sharp claws for all to see. While they did that, the man lay down on ground. A two-syllable word was uttered, and they spun on their heels, and commenced to acrobatically jump over the man. 600 lbs of jet and orange (or albino) fur flew over him in lethal sequences. Their wild scent stained the air. Excitement grew in the hearts of the crowd. The giant black man had supreme control over these animals. Words or gestures caused shocking actions. They purred like kittens or swatted each other in mock fights. At one point, he had them wearing church hats, complete with gauzy veils and flowers. At another point, they leapt in the air, catching and devouring the bloody chunks of meat he flung in the air.

At the end of the performance, both Sambo and his beasts stood up for a bow. This bought the audience to its feet.

Sambo looked up at his audience, and with the first grin of the evening—revealing unnaturally white teeth—he ran and opened the door to the cage.

He ran to the front, and with a flourish, announced his name: "Sambo!" But the way he pronounced it was unexpected. It came out sounding French. Like flambeaux.

Catch A T(n)ig(g)er...

Heat, particularly Southern heat, weights on the psyche like a heavy blanket. Sleep and stillness are the best remedies, for most.

But to Simba, the heat was a living thing. The cinder smell, the slipping past of hidden life, the whispering breezes, they all awoke within him memories of the jungle, dripping with bugs like jewels, the raucous squawk of flaming parrots, the chattering of the monkeys, all played before him in phantasmal splendor. He became restless, the hunting instinct alive in his flesh. The other beasts in his cage were born captive; he alone had once prowled the pulsing Indian night, before men came with nets and chains. Tonight, the dream jungle called to him.

He stood up, alerting his sleeping kin in the adjacent cages, who lazily acknowledged him with cinnamon glares. He shook himself, and padded over to the soiled side of the cage, and relieved himself. He snuffed the air, peered into the violet-tinged dark all of his kind perceived. And Simba sensed an anomaly. The door to the cage, normally tightly shut and padlocked, was not right. Metal did not rest comfortably against metal, as it usually did. Instead, there was a warp, yawning curve. The padlock was there, but it hung there uselessly, as did the flaccid silver snake of chain.

Simba padded over to the lopsided door, and investigated the area with sniffs and whisker-measuring. He walked back and forth several times, testing, exploring. After all, there could be a trap, a trick. Genes for caution pushed against the genes of adventure. He pushed his head through the gap, and found that it fit. He pushed it out of the gap, and the door snapped shut—and then slowly, swung slightly ajar. Simba coiled his strength, and forced his head through again, this time with force, and felt the give. The metalsnake protested, but not too loudly. Simba pushed again, and felt a groan through the bars. His kin stood up, and gave questioning sub-vocalizations. He answered with a push and growl that left his body half in and half out of the cage.

Simba was stuck. And he stayed stuck, while outside, the night danced beyond his reach. He struggled against his net of iron for a while, scraping himself, stretching himself into forms he did not know he could hold, until, finally, he was free, if slightly bruised. The other two tigers gave their tacit approval, and he melted into the night. He was no longer a tiger. He was a Tyger.

The white tyger slipped beneath the tent, and onto the darkened midway. The spoils of man, his wrappers, popcorn and flyers littered the path. He slunk close to the ground. He found a half-eaten sausage sandwich, which he devoured in less than two seconds. He looked up in the sky, and saw the clouds part, and saw the light in the sky whose color he half shared. The carnie trailers were silent, their lights out. He moved on, silent as shadow that was the color of his other half. Rats scurried and bolted from him. What little grass there was rustled at their escape. During his scouting, the tyger passed by a lone dog, a fellow competitor in night hunting. The cur started at the sight of the big cat. A bark began in its throat, then froze there. Simba's green eyes caught the moon, and flashed in seeming approval. The cur trotted away, towards the quiet trailers.

The tyger headed towards the fence that hemmed in the perimeter. It stood solid, as his metal cage had not. He galloped its length, seeking a weakness. There—where the stray dog had got in the grounds. The hole in the fence was too small for such as he. Besides, he was not too keen on repeating the night's earlier bruising birth. He turned away, turned back. Still—it was flimsy, here where the dog made his entrance. Perhaps— Maybe—

Simba launched at the makeshift fence. 650 pounds of muscle and intent cracked it wide open, with a loud snap. The noise almost was enough to disturb sleep. But the thick heat dulled reflexes. Naps resumed. One insomniac geek was startled as he imbibed morphine, and swore as soon as he finished, he'd investigate. But the unfurling tendrils of the drug lulled him into blissful stupor, freeing his mind from thoughts of bloody feathers.

Meanwhile, the tyger was free, and exulted in this newfound sensation. True, this sleepy hamlet was no jungle (the stink of man was everywhere), but it awoke long dormant instincts and abilities. A small wood at the periphery of town beckoned. He doused himself in its vegetable dankness. Simba stood still for a moment, just listening, tasting and testing the wholeness of it all. An owl hooted in some nearby tree. A cluster of bats flutter-flapped between the trees, with their tiny screeches. A lone pigeon soared and was silvered by the moon. Somewhere, a skunk flatulated. The ammonia smell assaulted his nostrils; it was time to move on.

Striding through the undergrowth, he remembered the dance of life and death in the jungle. The decay, the gases, the surging movement.

A rustle to his right, the flash of a hare. He took off after the bounding thing. No antelope, but it ran and consented to the game of the hunt. He swerved, and caught the pitiful thing. It practically leapt into his jaws in terror. He was merciful, snapped its neck and paid homage to its life by ingesting it—meat, blood, bones and all.

During his first night of freedom, he killed two more creatures of the unjungle (a squirrel and a possum) before he found a suitable place for a quick nap. He purred as he surrendered to sleep.

"Mumma, there's a munster in the woods."

Caro turned to face her dirty son, with his sweat-slicked hair and mud encrusted overalls.

"Baby doll, we've been over this a million times. There's no such things as monsters."

Caro turned back to the stove, and gave the simmering liquid a stir.

"But, Mumma," Jason said, "this monster's real."

"I'm sure it is, darling." She didn't turn around; she was mesmerized by the bubbling pattern on the surface of the syrup. "Now, you just go along and play. Or least, take a bath."

"But…."

Caro spun around. She noticed for the first time how he trembled. Maybe some wild animal had gotten in the woods, or a hobo.

"Alright. Where's the culprit?"

He pointed out the back door, towards the wooded area where the creek ran.

"OK, little man, let's have a look-see."

Jason stepped further away.

"Oh, come now. You can't be all that frightened. After all, you are mother's little man. And you're not going to let your mother go outside all by herself." She turned off the stove—the soft ball stage was just coming up, but she could make her White Divinity later.

Jason tentatively stepped forward. His mother grabbed his hand, and together they propelled forward, through the door and into the backyard. The heat was awful, and everything, even the air, was moist; it was as if everything was wrapped in chamois. Caro's heels had feeble purchase on the ground. She made a mental note to ask that colored man (Moe? Joe?) to take care of the lawn.

"Where's your monster, mister?"

Jason waved a chubby paw at a particularly dense patch of foliage. Caro shaded her eyes against the sunlight, and only saw shadows in the matted distance. They stood together, silent for the length of a monster's breath, and heard birds twittering and crickets chirping—the pizzicato of summer. And focusing, she heard—

Breathing? Heavy, asthmatic, purring…

She glanced at her son, who glanced back with You hear it, too? A tense, sullen watching and waiting.

Stupidly, she asked, "Who's there?"

There was no reply. Save, maybe, a snapping branch. It was as loud as a thunderclap. Jason jumped back.

"Sweetie, why don't you go back inside."

"Mm…mm," said Jason. Poor thing, he couldn't even say her name.

"Momma will be right behind you."

She glanced to him, watching his chubby legs carry him to the back door. In response to the fleeing child, the forest crashed, and out of it burst the monster. It was huge, the color of White Divinity, striped with licorice. Caro saw white fangs, the awful strawberry color of its mouth, and felt on his face its wild stench. It was Death, and it was chasing her little man.

"Run!" she screamed.

Jason reached the door, and wisely closed it. Caro was hit by a wave of relief—her baby was safe! But after that crested, a wave of fear rose in its place. She'd never felt anything like it. The heat of the day left; she could have been standing in Antarctica. She was bone cold. The beast turned away from the house, and faced her. The eyes were emerald green, set with in the mask of its face. How could evil be so white, and so beautiful? The tiger—for that was what it was— stood still, sniffing the air, sniffing her.

When she gave herself up to the fear, it was almost euphoric. She screamed as if ravished. Her panties soaked with wetness as if she'd been aroused. A final wave, of blackness, covered her, as she watched the tiger approach her. She fell towards the ground, in the throes of an enchanted sleep.

The blackberry bush was not too deep in the woods. Thoughts of his mother's cobbler made Ernest recklessly crash through the undergrowth, startling birds and, at one point, a rabbit. Dust rose up and collected on his overalls. He could hear Mama now, scolding him about how long it took to beat the dirt out of it. And Daddy gently reminding Mama that he was just a boy, and that boys are naturally dirty. Mama would throw her hands up, while he and Daddy chuckled.

It was hot and humid; this meant, in his short experience, that the berries would be plump and juicy. He turned off the path to where the grove of bushes proliferated. A white tiger lay in the shade of the bushes. It was a tableaux of moonwhite, blackberry stripes, all framed by green. Ernest thought it was some magical visitation, that the tiger would lead him to some fairyland. Then he remembered that there was a white tiger at the carnival in town. The scene before him blurred, and he dropped his tin pail. The beast turned in his direction, stood up, stretched. The tiger yawned, revealing teeth and an endless red cave.

As Ernest started to run, he thought about how angry Mama would be about him losing the tin pail.

At first, the Azaleans didn't know what to make of it. The carnies were rather tightlipped about it. But the hordes of them, including the bearded lady, crocodile man, flamingo girl, midget couple, and of course, Sambo, were frantically scouring the landscape for something—that raised more than a few eyebrows. Then, what had happened to Caroline Crawley, and Ernest Gibney spread through the town like wildfire.

A monster was in their midst. Carolyn's hands had been almost disconnected from her arms, when she was protecting her boy. She was now a gibbering mess of morphine and wet bandages. Ernest had been found in the woods barely breathing. His left leg bitten, the wound tarblack, brown and bright red, and you could see through to bone. Sightings of the white tyger were frequent and unreliable. Sambo, disconsolately wandering the town, calling out in his basso profoundo, was a more common sight. Night and day he could be seen, in wooded areas, parks, Wisteria Heights, Clovertown and Darktown. Both man and tiger were ghosts that haunted Azalea. At first, people gave him a wide berth. If anyone could control the escaped beast, he could. But when Ernest died of a fever, Sambo was no longer tolerated. Women in Darktown would chase him away with curses and Bible verses. He moved passed the crowd, oblivious, a messiah spurned. Folks in Clovertown threw bottles at him; Sambo ignored them, even when glass cut him. Swarms of children and teenagers followed the black giant, chanting childish songs:

Eeny, meenie, miny moe,
Catch a tiger by the toe...

Sometimes another word was substituted for 'tiger.' He still ignored them, a shadow passing through their midst.

Mobs from all corners of Azalea formed one night. They scoured the humid night with their torches and guns. Their paths crossed at the bank of the creek where Ernest had been attacked. Black, white, Irish Catholic and Protestant. Wordless, they joined into one mob, leaving mutual distrust and hatred behind, blending it into one whole with a single target.

The night sweated their prey into existence: the giant and the tiger were by the creek. The tiger had been chained around the neck by his master, who gave harsh commands in French that it sullenly obeyed. The demon and his familiar.

A low growl alerted Sambo to look up. He paused, while the tiger strained at the leash. The crowd spread out on the bank in a semicircle. Torchlight starred the dark water behind them. Guns angled towards man and beast.

One of the crowd said, "Ernest died."

They waited in silence while Sambo absorbed this news. A most unexpected thing happened at that moment. Sambo's fierce face fell and crumbled. Tears welled up in his eyes, and he began to sob. His body shuddered with grief. "Pauvre garcon," he said between tears. Confused men shuffled in the mud, and lowered their guns and torches. Some men removed their caps, and mopped their glistening faces with them. Sambo's anguish was genuine and affected the crowd deeply. The period of communal grief, led by the howling giant, lasted no more than a few minutes.

But someone broke the spell. "Your creature also harmed an upstanding citizen, not just a nigra child." His sentiment was echoed by others as grief gave way to rage. Guns were raised again. The castanet clicking of their cocking resounded through the night. Torches licked the night and set the gasoline-tension on fire. The tiger sensed this, and yowled. Muscle coiled and it lunged, breaking free of his master's leash.

A gun cracked, and the tiger fell like a piece of the night on the river's bank. Blood poured on the ground, and Sambo ran to the felled beast. He muttered in French, as he cradled the tiger, immune to the stench of voided bowels, the mud and the blood. They grabbed the sobbing giant, putting a noose around his neck and pulled him like an animal on a leash. They hung him in a tree. The branch broke as he crashed down. It took three different branches until they found the right one. The mob watched the absurd dance of his feet as breath left him, and his face turned purple as blood veins burst. When Sambo died, his eyes were open and filled with blood.

The mob then cut the body down, and laid it on the corpse of the tiger. They set both on fire. The smell of roasting meat rose and flavored the air. Embers hovered in the air like fireflies before they were faded out.

Sambo, like flambeaux.

If He Hollers, Let Him Go

Fiorelli's Carnival packed up quickly and left Azalea one night. They left a dusty plain, full of flyers and piles of dung. A fury of flies descended on the area, black and jeweled, as heat radiated from the ground. The entire area stank, of rotten food, stale air, urine and excrement. The grass had withered in the area, leaving it barren. Not even animals visited the site. For its part, Azalea went on as if nothing had happened. Meanwhile, the heat rose and rose. Mercury fingers went beyond the 90s, while humidity crushed and flattened everything down.

In the woods, a pile of ash and bones fused underneath the merciless heat. Asia and Africa, man and beast, Sambo and Simba. It joined with particles floating in the air, both psychic and corporeal. Guilt and grief, murder and madness, wonder and terror. Ash and bone crumbled into powder, imbued with a strange energy. In the hot siftings, something rose.

A new freak was born.

It stood up from the grey sand. Manshaped, its dark skin was wounded with white. The black stump of a tongue protruded from a violent purple head. Flames outlined the body. Flames that writhed but didn't burn. More tiger than man, it stalked the night. It visited the dead village of the carnival. Drowsy flies, drunk from manure and old food, rose and left the scene in swarms as the freak walked the area. Its flames surged before it vanished.

It began stalking Azalea—its new hunting ground.

Acknowledgments

Thanks to everyone who supported me and this avocation of mine. Here are my props: Ashe Journal, Gwenda Bond, Matt Cheney, Clarion West 96, Ellen Datlow, Sven Davison, Samuel Delany, Peter Dube, Thomas Drymon, Chip Gidney, Evan Gidney, Robert Guffey, Elizabeth Hand, Tanith Lee, Christopher Rowe, Rebel Satori Press, Tiffany Ricci, Serendipity.

And, of course, the kindness of Steve Berman and Lethe Press.

Lethe Press is pleased to donate 10% of its profits from sales of this book to the Carl Brandon Society.

About the Carl Brandon Society

The idea for the Society first came about at the feminist science fiction convention, WisCon, in response to a request from people of color in the community by scheduling more programming items that addressed race, and by having a focus group where people of color could meet and formulate strategies for increasing the awareness and representation of people of color in the genres and in the community. The Carl Brandon Society publish lists of speculative fiction written by people of color. Among their goals is working to make fandom a more pleasant place for people of color.

For more on the Carl Brandon Society, including membership, their awards, and how to donate to this worthwhile cause, please visit www.carlbrandon.org.

About the Author

A recent finalist of the Gaylactic Spectrum Award for Best Short Story, Craig Laurance Gidney is a graduate of the Clarion West workshop. His fiction has appeared in *Spoonfed, Say...Have You Heard This One?*, Ashé, and the anthologies *Magic in the Mirrorstone, Madder Love* and *So Fey.*

His book reviews have appeared on the online sites Bookspot Central and the blog The Mumpsimus. He lives in his native Washington, D.C. with two roommates and two cats.

CPSIA information can be obtained
at www.ICGtesting.com
Printed in the USA
BVHW031559071219
565887BV00001B/66/P

9 781590 210666